"I couldn't imagine a woman who'd be a good fit for you.

"You're a pretty private person, Jack Devon." His face was so close to hers, it was all Emily could do not to jerk away. Or lean in and kiss him.

"Do you think you're a good fit?" he teased.

"I swore I'd never date anyone from the company again. Plus I don't know a thing about you."

"Wrong. You know I can out ski you." His lips moved across her cheek, not kissing, just touching. "You know I respect your business judgment. You know I can cook."

"Sort of." Her breath hitched in her throat as his mouth moved to the edge of hers. "I've only seen you make garlic bread."

"And you know that kiss in the kitchen the other night wasn't just to prove a point. You know you kissed me back and enjoyed it way more than you're willing to let on. And you're willing to do it again."

D0594907

Dear Reader,

Here is an acronym that explains why you should not miss the opportunity to enjoy four new love stories from Silhouette Romance so close to Valentine's Day:

L is for the last title in Silhouette Romance's delightful MARRYING THE BOSS'S DAUGHTER six-book continuity. So far, Emily Winters has thwarted her father's attempts to marry her off. But has Daddy's little girl finally met her matrimonial match? Find out in *One Bachelor To Go* (#1706) by Nicole Burnham.

O is for the ornery cowboy who's in for a life change when he is forced to share his home…and his heart with a gun-toting single mom and her kids, in Patricia Thayer's *Wyatt's Ready-Made Family* (#1707). It's the latest title in Thayer's continuing THE TEXAS BROTHERHOOD miniseries.

V is for the great vibes you'll get from Teresa Southwick's *Flirting With the Boss* (#1708). This is the second title of Southwick's IF WISHES WERE… terrific new miniseries in which three friends' wishes magically come true.

E is for the emotion you'll feel as you read *Saved by the Baby* (#1709) by Linda Goodnight. In this heartwarming story, a desperate young mother's quest to save her daughter's life leads her back to the child's father, her first and only love.

Read all four of these fabulous stories. I guarantee they'll get you in the mood for *l-o-v-e!*

Mavis C. Allen
Associate Senior Editor

Please address questions and book requests to:
Silhouette Reader Service
U.S.: 3010 Walden Ave., P.O. Box 1325, Buffalo, NY 14269
Canadian: P.O. Box 609, Fort Erie, Ont. L2A 5X3

One Bachelor To Go

NICOLE BURNHAM

Marrying
The Boss's
Daughter

SILHOUETTE *Romance*®

Published by Silhouette Books

America's Publisher of Contemporary Romance

If you purchased this book without a cover you should be aware that this book is stolen property. It was reported as "unsold and destroyed" to the publisher, and neither the author nor the publisher has received any payment for this "stripped book."

Special thanks and acknowledgment are given to Nicole Burnham for her contribution to the MARRYING THE BOSS'S DAUGHTER series.

For Leah Vroman and Melissa Manley who listened. Thanks for laughing and commiserating at all the appropriate moments.

 SILHOUETTE BOOKS

ISBN 0-373-19706-3

ONE BACHELOR TO GO

Copyright © 2004 by Harlequin Books S.A.

All rights reserved. Except for use in any review, the reproduction or utilization of this work in whole or in part in any form by any electronic, mechanical or other means, now known or hereafter invented, including xerography, photocopying and recording, or in any information storage or retrieval system, is forbidden without the written permission of the editorial office, Silhouette Books, 233 Broadway, New York, NY 10279 U.S.A.

All characters in this book have no existence outside the imagination of the author and have no relation whatsoever to anyone bearing the same name or names. They are not even distantly inspired by any individual known or unknown to the author, and all incidents are pure invention.

This edition published by arrangement with Harlequin Books S.A.

® and TM are trademarks of Harlequin Books S.A., used under license. Trademarks indicated with ® are registered in the United States Patent and Trademark Office, the Canadian Trade Marks Office and in other countries.

Visit Silhouette at www.eHarlequin.com

Printed in U.S.A.

Books by Nicole Burnham

Silhouette Romance

Going to the Castle #1563
The Prince's Tutor #1640
The Knight's Kiss #1663
One Bachelor To Go #1706

*The diTalora Royal Family

NICOLE BURNHAM

is originally from Colorado, but as the daughter of an army dentist grew up traveling the world. She has skied the Swiss Alps, snorkeled in the Grenadines and successfully haggled her way through Cairo's Khan al Khalili marketplace.

After obtaining both a law degree and a master's degree in political science, Nicole settled into what she thought would be a long, secure career as an attorney. That long, secure career only lasted a year—she soon found writing romance a more adventuresome career choice than writing stale legal briefs.

When she's not writing, Nicole enjoys relaxing with her family, tending her rose garden and traveling—the more exotic the locale, the better.

Nicole loves to hear from readers. You can reach her at P.O. Box 229, Hopkinton, MA, 01748-0229, or through her Web site at www.NicoleBurnham.com.

FROM THE DESK OF EMILY WINTERS

One
~~Six~~ Bachelor Executive To Go

Bachelor #1: Love, Your Secret Admirer

Matthew Burke—Hmm...his sweet assistant ~~clearly~~ has googly eyes for her workaholic ~~boss.~~ Maybe I can make some office ~~magic happen.~~

Bachelor #2: Her Pregnant Agenda

Grant Lawson—The guy's a ~~dead~~ ringer for Pierce Brosnan. Who ~~wouldn't~~ want to fall into his strong, protective arms!

Bachelor #3: Fill-in Fiancée

Brett Hamilton—The ~~playboy~~ from England is really a British lord! ~~Can I~~ find him a princess...or has he found her already?

Bachelor #4: Santa Brought a ~~Son~~

Reed Connors—The ~~ambitious~~ VP seems to have a heavy heart. ~~Only~~ his true love could have broken it. But where is she now?

Bachelor #5: Rules of Engagement

Nate Leeman—Definitely a lone wolf ~~kind of guy.~~ A bit hard around the edges, ~~but I'll~~ bet there's a tender, aching heart ~~inside.~~

Bachelor #6: One Bachelor To Go

Jack Devon—The guy is so frustratingly elusive. Arrogant and implacable, too! He's going last on my matchmaking list until I can figure out what kind of woman a mystery man like him prefers....

battling the same problem he'd faced all week. Emily dropped her voice so only Carmella could hear. "I take it this doesn't regard our distributor trouble?"

A look from Carmella told her all she needed to know. She'd rather it concerned the distributor.

"I thought we decided not to pursue this plan any longer?" Emily shot another quick look at her father to make sure his attention remained on his phone call, then focused on Carmella. "I know how badly he wants me to marry someone here at the company. Enough that he's willing to go behind my back to pester my own colleagues into asking me out on dates. But now that we've managed to set up all the eligible men—"

"Except Jack Devon."

"Except Jack Devon. I know." Emily resisted the urge to roll her eyes. Just mention of the man's name, let alone seeing him in the flesh each day at work, put her on the defensive, both professionally and emotionally. She and Carmella couldn't possibly find a match for him. Not only was he a league above everyone else in the company, having been named one of Boston's Fifty Hottest Bachelors by *Boston Magazine,* he kept his privacy fiercely guarded.

But since Jack would never ask her out—pressure from Lloyd Winters or not—she didn't have to worry about him. Just last month, she'd overheard Jack talking to her father about a dinner party Lloyd had thrown the night before. He'd had the audacity to refer to her—to her own father!—as a "spoiled rich girl." Her father had laughed, rather than defending her to Jack, making it all the more evident how desperate he was to find her a husband. She wasn't about to risk her professional reputation trying to play matchmaker for Jack on the off-chance that Lloyd could convince him to ask out his "spoiled rich girl" daughter.

"That's who we need to discuss, and before your meeting," Carmella whispered, then more loudly added, "Could you help me with something, Emily?"

One of the company's vice presidents, Brett Hamilton, chose that very moment to pass near Carmella's desk on his way to grab a cup of coffee. "You need help, Carmella?"

"Emily's got it," she smiled. Brett continued on his way, and Carmella grinned at Emily.

Emily shook her head, then threw a pointed glance toward the conference room to remind Carmella of her meeting. The older woman hurried ahead of Emily, down the wide hallway between offices and past the desks of the myriad administrative assistants, then ducked into the women's room. After ensuring the stalls were empty, Carmella took a deep breath. "I know you were never comfortable with our plan to find girlfriends—or as it worked out, brides—for any of Wintersoft's bachelors, let alone for Jack Devon—"

"It's not my style to barge into anyone's personal life." Not only was it rude, she had other items on her to-do list. Like attending the sales meeting.

"Of course not. But we both know why it had to be done." Carmella jerked a thumb in the general direction of Lloyd's office. "If we didn't do it, it would have been done for us. And you wouldn't have liked the results. I saw what happened the last time your father pressured you into dating someone from the company.'' Carmella's eyes held a tinge of sadness. ''Todd Baxter did a number on you—and not just on your career.''

''Okay, so we didn't have a choice,'' Emily admitted. As much as she despised using personal information—gleaned from the company's personnel files, thanks to Carmella—about her co-workers to find them potential girlfriends before Lloyd pushed them into asking her out, she cared about protecting her heart and her reputation more—not to mention her father's reputation.

Lloyd Winters was a well-respected man and dedicated to his company, but both Emily and Carmella knew he had a huge blind spot where his daughter was concerned. One that, in the past, caused him to act against his own professional interests if he thought it would make Emily happy.

Or laugh when someone referred to his daughter as spoiled.

But in this case, finding Emily a husband—one who worked for Wintersoft and loved the company as much as she did—wasn't what would make her happy. Try as she might, Emily couldn't convince her father of that, even after the Todd Baxter disaster.

''I'll admit, our matchmaking plan worked out for the best for everyone. Five couples are living their happily-ever-afters, thanks to us.'' Emily leaned toward the door, making sure no one approached. ''But our role in those relationships is over and done with, so I don't think we should be talking about it anymore. If anyone finds out what we did—''

''That's why I dragged you in here. I think Jack Devon *has* found out.''

Emily set her cup down on the rest room's green-and-black granite countertop hard enough to splash coffee over the edge. Anyone but Jack! ''He has? How? I mean, he's given me some strange looks, and we know he suspects someone's gone through the personnel files, but he can't possibly know for certain—''

''Your father wants you to meet him in his office this morning at nine. He was adamant that you finish up the marketing meeting in time.'' Carmella's eyes widened in panic. ''He said it's important.''

Emily's breath gushed out in relief. She checked her watch, then picked up her coffee cup, glad the detour to the ladies' room wouldn't make her noticeably late for the sales meeting. She'd only been the Senior Vice President of Global Sales for less than a year, and she didn't want anyone to question her ability to handle such an important position. ''Carmella, you're seeing ghosts. You of all people should know my dad likes to have meetings on his own schedule. And that he thinks everything is important.''

Carmella's graying black hair bounced as she shook her head. ''No, this is different. Jack arrived very early this morning, before you got to work. He went straight to your father's office and waited for him to arrive, and their conversation sounded pretty intense. Jack told your father something that made him want to schedule a meeting—for all three of you—as soon as possible. Something's up. Something Jack started, not your father."

Emily tried not to let her alarm show on her face. "My dad was on the phone trying to close that deal with the new distributor when I walked by your desk. It could have something to do with that." Though, as Vice President of Business Development and Strategy, Jack would naturally be involved in hammering out partnerships with new distributors, both she and Carmella both knew that a contract dispute wouldn't be something Emily would handle as part of Global Sales.

"We'll see. I have a bad feeling." The lines in Carmella's forehead deepened as she spoke. "If Jack told your father that someone's been snooping in his personnel file, there'll be hell to pay. Your father's determined to find you a husband, someone who cares about the company as much as you do. If he found out I interfered in that, well, he trusts me more than you could ever know, Emily. I'd die if—"

"Then I'll take the blame." Emily put a comforting hand on Carmella's shoulder. In the ten years since Emily's mother had passed away, Carmella stepped into the role of nurturer in Emily's life as best she could. After twenty-five years as Lloyd's secretary—first at an investment banking company and the last twelve years at Wintersoft—Carmella knew the Winters family better than anyone. By the same token, Emily knew Carmella would be devastated if Lloyd discovered she had gone behind his back, even for a good reason.

"Just be careful," Carmella warned.

"I will." With Jack Devon in the room, how could she be anything but?

"Emily, take a seat. Jack just gave me the most interesting bit of information."

Emily stood in the doorway of Lloyd's spacious office, which overlooked Boston's financial district. He looked past Emily, then fixed his gaze back on her face. "Perhaps you should shut the door so we don't bother Carmella?"

Oh, no. Emily's gut seized in foreboding. Perhaps Carmella was right after all.

Emily turned to close the door, pinning Carmella with a private look that said, *Don't worry—yet.* Then, plastering a smile on her face, she strode across the polished hardwood floor and pulled out one of the two leather seats facing her father's desk. Since Jack Devon's long, powerful body occupied the other, she shifted her chair as far toward the opposite corner of her father's desk as possible.

Her nerve endings sizzled, as they often did around Jack. Ever since she'd seen *The Last of the Mohicans,* Emily's heart beat faster for Daniel Day-Lewis. The actor who'd portrayed the dark, mysterious Hawkeye in the movie stole her breath the moment he appeared on the screen.

Problem was, Jack Devon was Daniel Day-Lewis magnified. He possessed the same jet-black hair and high cheekbones that set her hormones afire, yet Jack stood taller, was more heavily muscled, and his skin bore a deeper tan than Lewis's, set off to perfection by his intelligent gray eyes. Despite his affable nature, an aura of the unknown clung to Jack like a dark cloak, and the fact she and Carmella had found so little in his personnel file to shed light on his background made him even more mysterious.

Worst of all, unlike a screen star—someone otherworldly, to be admired from afar—Jack Devon was a living, breathing, in-her-world-every-day male. And not only was he the most fabulous-looking male at Wintersoft, Emily guessed him to be the brightest. About the only thing she and Carmella knew for certain about him was that he'd attended Amherst on a full scholarship, then graduated near the top of his class.

Well, and that he considered her a rich, spoiled brat. She'd be better off to remember that.

Emily scooted her chair back another inch or two so she'd have space to think without Jack's presence clouding her brain. "So, Dad, what was this interesting tidbit?" And please, don't let him say Jack thinks someone has been digging in his personnel files. Someone like me. Or Carmella.

Lloyd gestured to Jack, who leaned forward in his chair, eliminating most of the space she'd managed to put between them. But instead of the accusatory look Emily expected, Jack's eyes lit with excitement, like those of a child about to unveil a surprise.

"There's a sizeable conference being held next week in Reno. I take it you've heard about it?"

Of course she had. "For the World Financial Services Organization, right?"

"Right." Lloyd interrupted, tapping a pen against a notepad on his desk as he spoke. "And Jack thinks—I think—you two need to take a trip out there."

You two? The last thing she'd expected to be given at this meeting was an airline ticket—particularly one of a pair that included Jack. Emily shot her father a questioning look. "We received the literature on that conference months ago. When I called, I was told the exhibitor booths have been reserved for nearly two years. Without a formal presence, I'm not sure how much we'd accomplish. A little networking, nothing more."

"That was my understanding, too," Jack said. "But when I was cleaning my desk last night, I made a follow-up call before trashing the brochures to put us on the list for the next conference, if nothing else. I learned that three exhibitors had cancelled. It's very late notice for us to prepare, but Acton Software grabbed one of the free booths day before yesterday, so—" He swung his focus to Lloyd. "You know what that means."

Emily turned to her father. "If we manage to snag a booth, we can demonstrate the beta version of Wintersoft's financial software, let the industry know it'll be ready to roll out in a couple months, and maybe pick up a few new clients—or at least keep our current ones from switching to Acton when their new software hits the market.''

"Precisely.'' Lloyd's blue eyes sparkled, and he tapped his pen against the top of his desk as he spoke, something Emily knew him to do whenever work pumped him full of adrenaline.

Wintersoft's biggest competitor, Acton Software, had already started taking orders for their newest financial services software suite—and offered heavy incentives for Wintersoft users to switch. Unless Wintersoft could prove to their current clients that the new Wintersoft program surpassed Acton's, they'd be in for a rough ride financially. This was their chance to offer that proof.

"I think we can swing it,'' Jack's confidence matched Lloyd's. "What's your schedule look like, Emily?''

Anticipation and wariness mingled in her brain as she tried to think through her schedule. "I'll clear it. This is too important to miss.''

Of course, attending the conference would mean a lot of late nights at work over the coming week, trying to prepare a rock-solid presentation, followed immediately by five days alone with Jack, working in close quarters at a trade-show booth.

At least it wasn't five nights. Thank goodness she'd be able to decompress in her own quiet hotel room each night.

"Great.'' Lloyd pushed back from his desk, then strode to his door and poked his head out. "Carmella, could you come in for a moment?''

Carmella entered, and Emily immediately sensed Jack's curiosity at the secretary's uncharacteristic nervousness.

Lloyd dropped into his high-backed leather desk chair and pulled the paperwork on the conference from a stack of folders on the edge of his desk. "I need you to book two tickets to Reno for Jack and Em. They'll be attending this conference next week."

Carmella took the information and studied it while Lloyd addressed Jack and Emily. "If you can have a list of your audiovisual needs to Carmella by tomorrow, she can call the hotel to make arrangements."

Emily started scribbling down the necessary items until Jack's voice interrupted her thoughts.

"I realize the El Dorado and Silver Legacy, which are across the street from the exhibition hall, are already booked solid. But don't you think staying in town is better, even if it's down the street at Harrah's or another hotel?"

Emily's head snapped up. Better than what?

Lloyd shook his head, and the determined set to his mouth set off Emily's warning bells. "I know it's a good forty-minute drive from Reno to my house, but the cabin is completely wired. I already have the beta version of the software loaded onto the computer if you need to access it or refine your sales presentation once you're there. I can get updates from you and Emily each morning before you head back to the trade-show floor. Plus, I won't have to worry about trying to track you down in two separate hotel rooms, and you won't need to deal with using a hotel business center, where the folks from Acton are sure to be lurking—''

Emily blinked. ''Whoa, Dad. You want us to stay at the house in Tahoe?'' *Together?* Granted, her father was right, in that the Winters' vacation home boasted every amenity a business traveler might need. But staying with Jack in such an intimate setting… The trade show would keep them busy during the day, but there wouldn't be a lot to do in the evenings. Not enough to keep their conversations focused solely on business.

Thanks, but no thanks.

If Jack had the faintest suspicion she or Carmella had poked into his personnel file, he'd be able to interrogate her without anyone else present. And even if he didn't, she wasn't sure she could handle five straight days—and nights—of having six-plus-feet and nearly two hundred pounds of heart-stopping, brain-fogging testosterone crowding her space. She could just picture herself padding downstairs in her flannel pajama pants, poking at the fire in the towering, two-story stone fireplace, then ambling over to the floor-to-ceiling windows to stare out at the snow-covered trees and the phenomenal blue surface of Lake Tahoe, only to have Jack walk up behind her.

She'd learned long ago—thanks to her father and his efforts to find her the perfect husband—that her professional life and her personal life needed to operate in separate spheres.

Unfortunately, her father hadn't learned that lesson, even after Emily's ex-husband, former Wintersoft golden boy Todd Baxter, had tried to steal company secrets. Emily wondered how much of her father's insistence that she and Jack stay at the Winters' place near Lake Tahoe had to do with convenience, and how much had to do with his hopes that his daughter might fall in love with the company's last remaining unmarried vice president, a man who'd conveniently stepped into the role of son-he-never-had in Lloyd's life once Todd's true nature had been revealed.

Emily's suspicions were confirmed by her father's wry grin. "You'll be far more comfortable at the house. And didn't you tell me just last week that we need to cut travel expenses? Well, this saves the company paying for two hotel rooms for a week, not to mention the costs of using the hotel business center, phone charges, room service—"

"All right," she conceded, unwilling to argue with her father in front of Jack and Carmella. Or tip off Jack to the fact that she was all too aware of his incredible body. "I take it you'll arrange to have the pickup waiting at the airport so we won't have to deal with a rental car?"

"Of course. I'm sure the Wilburs would be happy to drive it down and leave it for you," Lloyd answered, referring to the couple who kept things secure at his Tahoe home while he was working in Boston. "I'll have them check the firewood supply, stock the refrigerator, and take care of anything else they can think of."

"I'll call to let them know Jack and Emily's plans," Carmella assured him. She glanced once more

at Emily, her subtle look an indication she also rec-
ognized Lloyd's attempt to play Cupid, then returned
to her desk.

"Then everything's a go. Acton won't know what
hit 'em after you demonstrate the new software,"
Lloyd said over the rat-a-tat of his pen striking the
desktop. "I have complete faith in you two."

Emily gave her father a confident nod before leaving his office for her own. She'd have her work cut
out for her, preparing for the trade show—her first as
a company vice president—in less than a week. Quentin Kostador, the man who'd held her position before
her, usually spent two to three weeks getting ready.
But Emily knew the software and its selling points
cold, and she'd spent exhausting hours getting to
know each of the company's clients personally. She'd
wow them with the program's newest features, and if
Jack exuded half the charisma in a trade-show booth
he did at the office, new clients would be clamoring
to sign on, too.

She just hoped she could prepare herself for the
evenings as well as she could for their days.

A week with Emily Winters. Alone.

Jack closed his office door behind him and swore
under his breath. He'd forgotten all about the fact
Lloyd owned a home fit for an *Architectural Digest*
spread less than an hour from Reno. If he'd known
Lloyd would insist on having the two of them
stay there, he might've considered scrapping the
whole idea.

He exhaled and shucked off his black suit jacket, then looped it onto the hanger he kept on a hook behind his office door. No, Wintersoft had to have a presence at the trade show. There was no other way to keep Acton from cozying up to dozens of Wintersoft's clients, which included most of the world's top twenty financial services companies. He'd spent most of the last year putting in long hours convincing dozens of Wintersoft's major investors that the newest version of their software would save the financial services companies that made up Wintersoft's client base hundreds of working hours per year and revolutionize the way they did business. In turn, he'd argued, investors who poured their money into Wintersoft now, enabling the company to put all the necessary bells and whistles into the new software suite, would realize greater returns after it hit the market.

He wasn't about to disappoint those investors. And like it or not, there was no one who could rope in potential clients at the trade show as well as he could, with the possible exception of Emily Winters.

In his years at Wintersoft, he'd never worked a trade show with her. But she had to be good. Why else would she have been promoted to senior vice president at just thirty-one?

There was the daughter-of-the-boss reason, of course. He'd certainly known when he'd accepted the job at Wintersoft that he'd be working alongside Lloyd's daughter someday. No CEO in his right mind would overlook his Harvard-educated daughter when it was time to hire new employees. And he knew

Lloyd wasn't the type to promote an employee—any employee—without good reason.

Still, until he knew whether she could handle the wheeling and dealing of a trade show with the skill her predecessor, Quentin, had demonstrated, he'd keep an eye on her. As he had when Quentin was new, Jack figured he should handle any key contacts who happened by the booth himself. Just to be on the safe side.

After glancing at the red message light on his desk phone, he turned toward his window. Dealing with the business aspects of this trip would be the least of his problems. He had no desire to spend a solid week with Emily Winters—not if it was away from business, as hours alone at Lloyd's home would be. Something about her set his self-preservation instincts into overdrive. She and Carmella had been eyeing him and, he suspected, his personnel file. Why, he had no clue, and he didn't care. He'd long ago ensured it contained nothing of import.

But if his hunch was right, Emily would inevitably use the time they spent at Lloyd's house or commuting back and forth into Reno to try and wriggle personal information out of him. With those long legs of hers on display next to him all day long, or with her sultry, full lips sipping wine across the table from him over dinner every night, he'd be sorely tempted to forget his vow to keep business and pleasure separate.

As much as he hated to admit it, Emily Winters was the complete package—everything he'd ever desired in a woman—intelligence, a phenomenal body, ambition—and everything he couldn't have. Thanks to his parents' dysfunctional marriage, he knew serious relationships weren't for him. And Emily had Serious Relationships Only written all over her exquisite face.

He stretched his arms overhead, then forked his fingers through his hair, wishing he could clear his mind. Lust. That's all it was, lust clouding his judgment. How long had it been since he'd kissed a woman with a brain in her head? One who challenged him?

How long had it been since he'd kissed a woman at all?

He leaned his forehead against the cool glass of his window and stared down at Milk Street, nearly fifty floors below him. Raising his head, he looked off to the south, in the direction of the Quincy Shipyards and all that he'd left behind.

He had everything he wanted in life, except someone to share it with. But that was for the best. He'd worked too hard and too long to stand in a posh office like this—one that afforded him financial security and the means to pay back his mother for all she'd done—to allow loneliness or desire to screw it up. The last thing he needed was to allow himself to be attracted to a woman whose entire demeanor screamed Long-Term Commitment, the one thing he couldn't give a woman. Or for someone—even an attractive, intelligent someone—to pry into his personal life.

Because if Emily stumbled onto too much information, it could mean the end of his professional life.

Chapter Two

Emily's footsteps echoed against the linoleum floor as she made her way to the rear of the vast exhibition hall, where Jack busied himself making final preparations on Wintersoft's booth. Jack started at the sound of her approach, then eyed the plastic shopping bag clutched in her hand with hope.

They'd arrived in Reno several hours before, but rather than going straight to the house to drop off their suitcases and refresh themselves, they decided to check their setup in the exhibition hall first.

Emily suggested the pit stop to postpone the inevitable—being alone with Jack in her father's gorgeous mountain home—but the delay tactic ended up saving their tails. The staff at the exhibition hall hadn't connected the computers correctly, and the booth's backdrop wobbled. It hadn't taken long to find a crew at the hall to repair the backdrop, preventing the huge Wintersoft corporate logo and over-size screen mounted there from crashing down mid-demonstration, but troubleshooting the computer hookups was another matter. Three hours after Jack and Emily arrived in Reno they were still working out the final glitches.

"This should get the demo to display on the large screen as well as on the computer screens," Jack commented as he took the cable from Emily's plastic bag and pushed the prongs into the appropriate slot. "Where'd you get it?"

"Computer shop a few blocks from here. They did the work on my father's house, so I knew they'd have it." She frowned, studying the tables one more time. "I still have to wonder what happened to the cable Carmella sent. I saw her ship it myself."

"Wouldn't be surprised if someone else borrowed it," Jack grumbled.

Emily watched as he crawled under the table, the knees of his dark slacks gathering dust from the floor, and tried to ignore the fact the man had his backside in her line of sight.

Man, this was going to be a long five days of mean-ingless chitchat.

On the flight from Boston to Chicago, he'd napped, saving her the problem of concocting small talk. Then, on the leg from Chicago to Reno, he'd been all business as they'd run through the points they'd high-light in their demonstrations and rehearsed answers to questions comparing their new software suite to Ac-ton's. Though it didn't hurt to cover the information, they'd been ready to go yesterday, before they'd left work, and both of them knew it. The in-flight review session merely served to keep topics professional, instead of personal.

But now that dinnertime had arrived, the exhibition hall had emptied of others who'd come to double-check their booths. She and Jack might have been seated elbow-to-elbow on the airplane, but the solitude of the cavernous hall made her more aware of Jack's presence than sharing a row on their crowded flight.

And judging from his intense focus on the computer cables, he was equally aware of her. Why he felt that way, when he seemed perfectly at ease with everyone else in the company—and, according to *Boston Magazine,* with the town's female population—bothered her. If it was the files, then she wished he'd just forget it, or confront her and get it over with. On the other hand, if it was the same sexual attraction that hummed through her system every time he was within eyesight, she didn't want to know about it. No matter how devastatingly handsome Jack might be, an office romance—at least for her—meant nothing but trouble.

"I think it's set," he said, backing out from under the table. "Try it out."

Emily powered up the computer and clicked on the Wintersoft icon, willing the software to load faster. When it finally popped onto the screen, she typed in her password and the demo of the software's beta version appeared, waiting for her to click on Start.

Behind her, on the booth's backdrop, the same view appeared on the movie screen, large and crisp enough for passersby to watch the demonstration.

"Ve-e-e-ry nice," she drawled. "As long as it works at eight tomorrow morning, we're golden."

"It will." Jack brushed the dust from his slacks, then glanced around the hall. "Guess we're the last ones left."

Emily nodded as she shut down the computer and set a new password to prevent the curious from accessing the system before morning. "Just as well. Gave us a chance to check out Acton's booth without anyone giving us the eye."

Jack grunted his agreement. While Acton's setup was visually stunning and clearly designed to have more than two people manning the booth, Emily and Jack agreed that Wintersoft had done a better job on their sales materials and setting up a user-friendly demonstration area. In Emily's experience, financial services customers preferred substantive information over razzle-dazzle nine times out of ten.

"So," he ventured, "would you like to grab a bite here in Reno before we head up to the house? I'm assuming there are a few good restaurants nearby."

Emily mentally ticked off the nearby choices. Art Gecko's at Circus Circus was close, but usually had a line. There was a brew pub in the Silver Legacy, but it'd be smoke-filled by this late in the day. Her favorite restaurant, the Roxy Bistro, was closest of all, across the street in the El Dorado Hotel. With its soft alabaster lighting and sultry waitresses bringing martinis to candlelit tables, however, it'd be way too romantic. Better to face the discomfort of the drive and get it over with.

"It's getting late," she replied, hoping she didn't sound as though she'd given the decision more intense thought than it deserved. "I'm sure the Wilburs have stocked the fridge. Plus, with the snow, it'll be safer to drive up there before it gets too dark. And this way, we can get plenty of rest before tomorrow. We'll want to be here early."

Jack agreed—almost too readily. "I suppose most of the dinner places are in the casinos, anyway." He shouldered the bag full of presentation materials, then gestured toward the exit at the far end of the hall. "After you."

Thankfully, the drive wasn't as awkward as she'd feared. Since Jack had never before visited Reno or Lake Tahoe, she took the opportunity to point out the sights, but as they rounded the final curves on the road to the Winters' vacation home, her gut tightened in dread. Her escape—the home to which she'd retreated after her horrible divorce, the place she and her father found solace after Emily's mother died—suddenly didn't feel like an escape. Jack's presence would fill even the largest home.

"You must love coming up here," Jack whistled as Emily pulled off the main road and onto a smaller, dirt- and snow-packed one, the end of which lay hidden as it twisted toward the lake through a thick stand of ice-encrusted evergreens. Emily eased her father's red pickup truck to a stop at a low gate, then rolled down the window and punched in the security code that would swing the gate open.

"I do. You'll love the view. You can see Lake Tahoe from nearly every room in the house."

"Then it must be spectacular."

Minutes later, Emily unlocked the front door of the home, set her suitcase inside the entry, then waved Jack in behind her. She took a deep breath, reveling in the smell of the polished wood railings and the comfortable leather furniture. How many nights had she skipped going to bed altogether when she visited here, opting instead for the rich brown leather sofas in the living room, where she could indulge in a cup of hot cocoa before a crackling wood fire, allowing herself to get lost in the view across the water?

"I think spectacular is an understatement," Jack's rich voice came from behind her.

Emily turned and smiled at him, unable to help herself. "Want the grand tour?"

At Jack's grin, she swung her arm in a wide arc reminiscent of Vanna White. "This is the entry hall. Stairs down are in front of you. As you can see, we've actually entered on the second floor, since the house is built down the side of the hill."

She strode a few paces to her right and opened a large cherry door, but didn't go inside. Being in a bedroom with Jack in her own home, even as part of a business trip, would be too unsettling.

"You'll be staying in here. There's a full bath, and my dad keeps the medicine cabinet stocked for guests. Help yourself to anything you need. There are extra sheets in the linen closet, and a robe hanging on the back of the door.''

Jack stepped past her into the room and set down his suitcase. After taking off his jacket and tossing it over the suitcase, he poked his head in the bathroom door, fingering the thick white terry robe. ''Better than the Ritz.''

He glanced around the room, admiring the built-in cherry desk and the king-size bed, which faced a wall of glass looking out over the lake, before rejoining her in the entry.

''That's my room,'' she waved to a cherry door on the opposite side of the small entry hall. She hadn't intended to show him her room, but before she could stop him, he picked up her suitcase and carried it in for her, setting it at the foot of the bed.

Again, she kept to the doorway, unwilling to stand in a bedroom with him. ''It's pretty much identical to yours. The rest of the house is down here,'' she gestured to the staircase, between the two bedroom doors. Thankfully, he didn't linger in her room. The sight of him standing at the foot of her bed, studying the view out the row of windows with his hands on his hips, was an image she didn't want lingering in her mind.

He followed her down the staircase, admiring the wide pine steps and carved railing. When they reached the main floor, his head tilted back as he absorbed the sight of the two-story, double-sided stone fireplace set in the center of the open-space floor plan. Behind the fireplace, floor-to-ceiling windows boasted a breathtaking view of the sun setting over Lake Tahoe. To their left, next to the stairs, a galley kitchen with cherry cabinetry featured a state-of-the-art stove and refrigerator. A beige granite countertop separated the kitchen from the dining area, where a long, mission-style cherry table and eight chairs sat at an angle so guests could enjoy the stunning view out the windows and the warmth of the fireplace while they dined. An inconspicuous glass door near the table opened onto a balcony, the bottom of which just grazed the tops of the snow-dusted evergreens on the hillside below the house.

"Your father's architect must've been a brilliant guy," Jack commented. "The way the house fits against the hillside with windows on the exposed face, it makes you feel like you're part of the outdoors, but without the chill."

Jack admired the view in awe before turning to his right, where, five steps below them, the sunken living room's leather seating surrounded the opposite side of the fireplace. Nearer the windows stood an ebony baby grand piano. Photos of Emily, her parents, grandparents, and assorted cousins were scattered across the ledge, so anyone seated on the piano bench could enjoy them. Dominating the far wall of the living room, a computer with a large viewing screen sat in the midst of a built-in cherry wall unit filled with the latest high-tech equipment. Jack nodded toward the setup. "And I can see why your father insisted we stay here. We'd never have this kind of office support at a hotel."

Emily ignored the computer equipment, instead staring at the fireplace and the view beyond. For all its convenience, the fancy electronics were just an excuse for Lloyd to send them here. Across the lake, scattered lights appeared on the hillside amongst the evergreens, while pink and purple clouds dragged their thin fingers through the orange-colored sky overhead. *Romantic* didn't even begin to describe it. And her father knew it.

She turned back to Jack. "My father doesn't make any plans without thinking them through first."

Jack raised an eyebrow. "I hope that means he encouraged the neighbors to leave a little something in the refrigerator. I haven't eaten since that soggy sandwich on the plane."

"Me, either." Of course, knowing her dad, he'd probably asked the Wilburs to leave a bottle of champagne and chocolate-covered strawberries in the hope his daughter and Jack would indulge.

Emily strode to the fridge and opened the stainless-steel door. "Mrs. Wilbur—our nearest neighbor—left a jar of her homemade spaghetti sauce. She made us a casserole, too." Emily reached past the newly purchased asparagus bundle, a bag of apples, and a bottle of wine to pull a sticky note off the top of the casserole dish, then smiled at Mrs. Wilbur's familiar handwriting. "She says she knows she was only supposed to bring groceries from the list my father e-mailed her, but that she couldn't resist giving us some 'real' food."

Jack entered the long, narrow kitchen behind her,

and leaned a hip against the granite countertop. "She takes care of this place while you're in Boston?"

"She's great. Her husband, too." Emily offered Jack a soda, purposely ignoring the chilled wine to grab the can from the back of the fridge. She'd missed her guess with champagne, but not by much. The label identified it as her father's favorite Pinot Grigio, and she knew it hadn't been here on her last visit.

"So should we heat up the casserole?" Jack asked.

"We should probably save it for tomorrow, when we've been on the trade-show floor all day. But since Mrs. Wilbur left the sauce, I can make spaghetti, if you like."

One side of Jack's full mouth tweaked up. "You're going to cook while we're here?"

Such arrogance. "You bet. And so will you." She eyed a fresh loaf of Italian bread in a basket at the end of the countertop. "Think you can manage to turn that into warm garlic bread?"

"I think so."

Emily grabbed the box of pasta off the shelf, then located a pot and began filling it with cold water. She wondered how long she could keep the conversation on mundane things and off Wintersoft—and the files she and Carmella had accessed.

As he pulled a knife from the butcher block and squared the bread on a cutting board, Jack saved her the trouble. "You must have had a great family life growing up."

Was it her, or did his voice hold a hint of wistfulness? With her back to Jack, Emily turned the water on to boil. "What makes you say that?"

"This place. Your father wouldn't have built it if he didn't want to spend a lot of up-close-and-personal time with his family. There are only two bedrooms, one for you, and one for your parents. It's not the typical ski area vacation home, designed to sleep as many people as possible in as tight as space as possible."

He jerked his head in the general direction of the piano. "The pictures in the living room are a give-away, too. Most people don't take the time to personalize their vacation homes. They just treat them like fancy hotel rooms."

Emily agreed, thinking of the other homes in the area, but as she turned to search for a colander, she realized Jack had stopped slicing and was staring toward the piano with its family photos.

"You were very lucky," he added. His words were offhand, but his gray eyes held an unmistakable iciness.

Feeling a need to explain, Emily said, "My father worked as an investment banker when I was growing up. Very long hours. Even during our family vacations on Cape Cod, clients expected him to answer their calls immediately and drive back into Boston at the drop of a hat if they wanted something done. But when we came here on a ski trip once, his clients seemed to realize that he couldn't just pop into the office. We didn't get a single call. He figured out that if he wanted guaranteed time with my mother and me, this would be the place to build a vacation home. Not the Cape.''

"Aside from the obvious." Jack waved the bread knife in the direction of the windows.

Emily grinned. "My dad used to say coming here sent his clients a message."

"Do not disturb?"

"Precisely. We spent the Christmas holidays here every year, plus a week in the summer. More, when he could get away." She couldn't help but laugh. "Of course, my father still had the place wired to within an inch of its life. He can't live without his gadgets."

Jack finished spreading garlic butter on the slices of bread, then wrapped the entire loaf in aluminum foil and gestured for Emily to open the oven. "Here you go. My mother's famous garlic bread. Never let it be said an Irishwoman couldn't make a proper Italian meal. Or teach her son."

Emily leaned against the counter, surprised. In the time she'd spent around Jack in the office, she'd talked to him about which sports teams he liked, what kind of music he enjoyed, and, of course, about his personal thoughts on Wintersoft's various clients. But she didn't once recall him talking about his family. To anyone. In those few sentences, he'd given her more information about his background than Carmella had found in months of searching. More than she'd learned in years of water-cooler conversations. "You're close to your mom?"

He shrugged, then busied himself washing his hands. "She lives in Florida now."

"But when you were growing up?"

"My mom was great. Carmella tells me yours was wonderful, by the way. A very classy woman."

"She was." Though she'd passed away while Emily was in college, just over ten years ago, Emily missed her mother every day. And she couldn't walk through this house without noticing her mother's little touches. The painting of a flamenco dancer in motion that she'd picked up on a trip to Argentina. The ornately carved spice rack she couldn't resist buying for the kitchen. All the rugs and furniture, aside from the computer furniture, had been selected by her mother.

Realizing Jack had changed the topic on her, she asked, "What about your father?"

"He died several years ago."

"Oh. I'm sorry to hear that."

"No big deal." He glanced toward the stove. "Your water's boiling."

Emily turned away from Jack and dumped the spaghetti into the pot. She could take a hint. No more questions about his upbringing.

Though she and Carmella had wondered about it, strictly for purposes of their now-defunct matchmaking plan, tonight Emily found herself personally curious. Jack and his mother sounded close, but there'd obviously been problems with his father.

Well, she could understand that, too. She watched as Jack picked her father's favorite glass from the dozens in the cupboard, then added ice and poured his soda into it. She could just picture the grin on her father's face at his selection.

Emily knew that her father loved her dearly, but he'd always wanted a son. Someone like Jack, who might someday run the company. That was the main reason her father had encouraged her to marry Todd Baxter. Todd had been a golden boy at Wintersoft, and her father had always held him up as an example of the ideal company employee.

She forced back a sigh as she stirred the spaghetti. It wasn't that her father was sexist. He'd treated her just like any other employee at Wintersoft—giving her both the good and the bad during her yearly reviews, promoting her solely on a merit basis—but deep inside, she sensed, he'd wanted to leave his company to someone who'd carry on the Winters name. Someone who'd sit back and sip brandy with him late at night and talk business. And in her father's mind, that wasn't a daughter. So he'd hoped for second best—that his daughter would marry a man he could treat as a son, a man who'd fill a son's role in his company.

She wondered if Jack had figured out that facet of her father's personality. After all, Jack had been at Wintersoft during Emily's marriage—and divorce— from Todd Baxter. And Jack had been involved in the investigation just last month, when it was discovered that Todd had broken into the files on Wintersoft's new software suite with the intent of selling the information as a way of getting back at Emily and the company.

She glanced sideways at Jack. She'd done great work for Wintersoft, introducing innovative, successful sales strategies that had impressed her father enough to warrant her recent promotion. But did the explosion over Todd color Jack's views about her professionalism? Did her father's efforts to find her a husband give Jack the idea she might not be worthy of someday running the company, should she strive for that goal, let alone of handling tomorrow's trade show?

"Maybe we should talk about tomorrow," Emily said as she took the garlic bread out of the oven and put the warm loaf in a lined basket.

A vertical crease appeared between Jack's eyes. "I thought we covered it on the plane. Unless there's something I've missed?"

"Not missed, exactly. Something I just remembered. Do you know Randall Wellingby?"

"Heard of him. Last I heard, he'd been appointed to the board of directors for the Allied Banking Group over in the U.K."

"He's still on the board. But while you were napping on the flight, I caught up on reading the trade newsletters that have been piling up on my desk. Apparently, Wellingby's been appointed the head of ABG's New York office. So it's very likely he'll be attending the conference."

"ABG uses Acton Software." Jack took the plate of spaghetti Emily held out to him, and carried it to the table, along with the basket of bread. "You think he's open to switching?"

"Possibly. I visited our Frankfurt office last year, and managed an appointment with him during a layover in London. He said ABG was happy with Acton overall, but…'' She quirked her mouth as she handed Jack silverware and napkins. ''I got the feeling there were some issues between them. If Wellingby does make an appearance, we need to make sure he gets a good look at our new software. If he likes it and relations with Acton aren't exactly rosy, he's got the clout to switch ABG over to Wintersoft.''

They took their seats just as the sun's final rays disappeared behind the hills across the lake. ''Landing ABG would be incredible,'' Jack said as he fluffed his napkin and dropped it into his lap. He was quiet for a moment, then asked, ''What does Wellingby look like?''

Emily pictured Randall Wellingby as he'd sat across a table from her in the lounge at Heathrow Airport's business center. ''Tall. About six-three or -four, I'd guess. Blond hair. Good-looking guy. Very well-dressed. I'm guessing he's in his late thirties. Possibly early forties. With his height and looks he'll stand out, so we shouldn't miss him.''

An odd look flickered over Jack's face. Had she made a mistake by referring to Randall as good-looking?

''Okay,'' Jack replied. ''If I see him, I'll get him over to the booth and give him the demo.''

''He might be more comfortable with me, since I've already met with him once. We need every advantage we can get.''

Jack forked a bite of spaghetti into his mouth. After swallowing, he said, ''I suppose that's true.''

Emily looked down at her spaghetti, and tried to focus on twirling it around her fork. His tone didn't demonstrate much confidence. Did Jack think she had the hots for Randall? Or that she lacked the sales experience to close a deal with the well-known businessman?

Either way, she didn't like it. But since Jack hadn't come right out and said anything offensive, she let his odd look and comments slide. Ever since the Todd fiasco, she'd been overly sensitive about how others within the company viewed her.

She'd just have to make sure that when—if—Randall Wellingby made an appearance at the trade show, she went all-out to convince him to switch ABG to Wintersoft. Now that she headed up Global Sales, she'd be doing more and more of these trade shows. And there was no way she'd let Jack Devon believe she'd gotten her position based on anything other than merit. Even if she was her father's daughter. Or Todd Baxter's ex-wife.

Chapter Three

Jack tried not to glance at his watch as he waited for the doors to the exhibition hall to open. Registration for the World Financial Services Organization's conference started fifteen minutes earlier, meaning the first attendees through that line would be heading to the trade show any moment.

Adrenaline pumped through his veins as he tapped the keys to load the demo program, then waited for the Wintersoft graphics to pop onto the giant screen behind him. This was the best part of his job—the anticipation of nailing down a client, of wowing them with a product superior to anything else on the market.

Today, however, edginess blended with his usual excitement. He was used to having Quentin Kostador, a five-foot-eight, stocky, balding man, in the booth with him.

Jack took a deep breath as he focused his attention on the screen in front of him, purposely ignoring Emily, who stood to his right. As she set out sales materials sporting the Wintersoft logo along the booth's wide display table, every move showed off her legs, which were accented by the lean, just-over-the-knee black skirt she'd chosen to wear today.

Why couldn't she have worn slacks?

And why in the world was he feeling the least bit tempted by the boss's daughter?

He'd spent his whole career keeping business and pleasure separate. Very separate. As in, no relationships with women who'd want to encroach on his late-night working hours, let alone on his space. And no relationships intense enough that a woman might question his past.

It had worked so far. And he enjoyed dating around—finding women to accompany him to fundraisers and other must-do corporate events—until eight months ago, that is. One of his college classmates from Amherst, now an editor at *Boston Magazine,* spotted him out and about twice during the same week. First at Turner Fisheries, in the Back Bay, having dinner with a blond photographer before a Save the Children event he was attending on behalf of Wintersoft. Then having lunch at Davio's over in Cambridge with a petite brunette—a party organizer who was helping him with a Wintersoft event.

A month later, Jack realized his so-called friend had jumped to conclusions and stuck his name in at number twelve on the list of Boston's Hottest Bachelors, making Jack the focus of spicy office gossip.

Dating around lost its allure the moment he'd realized even a simple meal out—like those he'd previously enjoyed—might endanger his career.

Since then, he'd kept busy enough at work not to miss it. The only date he'd had since the article appeared was to a dinner at Lloyd's house, where he'd been obligated to bring someone. And even that turned out badly. He'd invited a model who he knew would be in town only temporarily. Though he'd only had to spend one evening with her, he'd found the girl to be vapid and spoiled rotten by her wealthy parents. Lloyd had even joked about her later at the office. Jack had covered, letting Lloyd know he wasn't serious about the "spoiled little rich girl." But it did make him wonder what Lloyd thought, especially when combined with the coverage Jack received from *Boston Magazine*—an issue of which he'd spied on Lloyd's desk.

But sharing a quiet dinner with Emily last night—seeing her vacation home, studying photos of her family, sleeping in a bed he guessed she'd slept in on previous visits—made him realize the void that article, and his privacy concerns, left in his life.

He kept his gaze averted from Emily. Who was he kidding? Even if he could manage to enjoy a decent date again, he'd never have an idyllic family life with a loving wife and children.

His damned father had ruined it for him. First when Jack was a child, and now, even in death. No matter how hard Jack worked at Wintersoft to obtain financial security, no matter how wonderful a woman he might meet, it could all be blown away in a moment if anyone learned the truth about Patrick Devon.

If he didn't blow it himself by following in his father's footsteps.

He closed his eyes for a moment, a wave of jealousy washing over him at the images his own childhood conjured when contrasted with Emily's. From seeing her around the office, watching her father dote on her and then promote her, he'd wondered if Emily had grown up as spoiled as his vapid date.

He'd realized early on—and the family photos reinforced his realization—that she hadn't. Rich, yes. But not spoiled. Loved and cared for, in a way his mother would have done if his father hadn't reduced them to living hand-to-mouth.

"Do you have the file on Metrogroup?" Emily's soft voice jerked him from unpleasant thoughts of his father.

"In my briefcase. Help yourself." He pointed with his elbow, fingers still on the keyboard. "It's got a blue tab on top."

Emily located it, reviewed the info, then slid it back just as the first wave of conference-goers poured into the hall. Within moments, Jack and Emily spied one of Metrogroup's information technology specialists making his way along the aisles of vendors.

"He looks familiar. Mike, right?" Jack whispered.

"Yep. Mike Elliott," Emily murmured as the man approached. "He contacted our help line twice last year. Both pretty basic issues, and we resolved them quickly. So he should be very happy with our current software. Getting him to upgrade to the new version, instead of going with Acton, should be a snap. Oh, and tomorrow's his birthday.''

Jack glanced at Emily, trying to keep the look of awe from his face. ''That's all in the file?''

Emily gave a slight nod, smiling at Mike Elliott as he approached the table. ''I updated it before we flew out.''

''I'm impressed,'' he managed under his breath, before extending his hand to Mike. ''Mike, Jack Devon. I believe we met last year.''

The heavyset man pumped Jack's hand. ''Jack Devon, of course. Glad to see Wintersoft here.''

Jack introduced Mike and Emily, then focused once more on Mike. ''Did you get the letter we sent out last month about our software upgrade? We'll be rolling out the new version next month, but we brought the demo to the trade show so you could try it out. It has some enhancements I think would benefit Metrogroup immensely. Would you like to take it for a spin?''

''They didn't send me to Reno for the gambling, unfortunately,'' Mike grinned, then allowed Jack to start the demonstration for him.

''What a way to spend your birthday. I seem to recall that it's this week.''

''It is.'' Mike looked surprised that Jack remembered, but as Jack began putting the program through its paces, testing out some of the new features, Mike said, "You know, Acton's offering some heavy incentives to switch. Are you guys willing to match their price?"

"I'm not sure what we can do on price," Jack admitted. "Obviously, for a client as large as Metrogroup, we're willing to do our best. But I think, when you compare our new software side-by-side with Acton's, you'll see that switching, no matter what the incentives, would be a mistake."

When Mike looked doubtful, Jack glanced at Emily, then added, "You only called our help line twice last year. And both times, we fixed the problem on the spot. That meant almost no downtime for Metrogroup, and as you know, no downtime means hundreds of thousands of dollars in savings to the company. I don't think Acton can promise that."

Emily smiled to herself, knowing she'd given Jack a grade-A example of her sales expertise. Good.

While Jack focused on highlighting features of the software upgrade to Mike, Emily turned her attention to the crowd. Several passersby had stopped walking to watch the software demonstration on the oversize screen. Emily moved to the front of the booth and encouraged them to ask questions, and within a couple of hours, managed to land a new client, in addition to convincing three current clients to stay put. Just as her stomach started to rumble in anticipation of lunch, she spied a blond head at the back of the crowd and moving forward.

"Randall, so nice to see you," she smiled as he

approached the table. "Heard you're in New York now. Congratulations!"

"Thank you, Emily," he greeted her in his thick British accent. "Wonderful to see you again, too. I really enjoyed our meeting in London."

Emily fought not to blush. Something in Randall's tone made her realize he meant it—he was truly happy to see her here.

"Well, since you're at my table, I'm hoping this means you've thought more about switching ABG over to Wintersoft?"

He leaned forward and picked up one of the brochures Emily had ordered from the printers as soon as she and Jack had decided to attend the trade show. "Depends on how convincing you are. But looking at this," he perused the brochure, then raised his eyes to the large screen behind her, "tempts me." His gaze shifted to her face. "The entire booth is tempting."

Emily put on her best business smile. "Well, I didn't manage to tempt you away from Acton during our London meeting, but I have a feeling that once you try out our new software, you'll want ABG to switch. Shall I give you the nickel demonstration?"

Since Jack had left the primary computer to talk to a representative from Outland Systems, one of Wintersoft's business partners, she eased Randall toward the display. The minute Randall stepped up to the keyboard, however, she felt Jack's gaze on her. She hazarded a glance over her shoulder, and met Jack's gray eyes. He was listening to the man in front of him speak, but it was obvious to her that he was equally interested in what she was doing.

Well, so what if he wanted to handle Randall himself? She was doing a good job, and if nothing else, landing ABG as a client would prove to Jack—and the rest of the company—that she belonged in her new position.

While Randall ran the demo, she described several scenarios where ABG could save money by using Wintersoft instead of remaining with Acton. Careful not to push too hard, she also made a point of chatting with Randall about his move and the adjustment he had to make living in New York as a lifelong London resident.

"This is truly fantastic," Randall commented as he finished running the demonstration. "And you say that we'll have access to your technical assistance staff twenty-four hours a day?"

"Twenty-four, seven," she promised. "But we hope you won't need it. As you know, Metrogroup uses Wintersoft. They look to accomplish many of the same tasks as ABG when it comes to using the program. Last year, they only called our help line twice, and both times we had the matter resolved in well under an hour. I won't ask how many hours your information technology department spent on the phone with Acton technical support in the last year, but I'm willing to bet it was more than that."

Randall raised an eyebrow. "Only twice? That's astounding."

Emily beamed with pride. How could she not, after

watching her father work so hard to earn Wintersoft its reputation? "Mike Elliott from Metrogroup is attending the conference. Ask him yourself. Or better yet, if any of your information technology specialists are here, send them to me. Have them try to crash the program. Won't happen."

"You're that confident?" He laughed. "I'll tell you what. You were right when we met in London. We have been having some trouble with the Acton software. Nothing major—they're a good, solid company—but I'm not convinced their upgrade offers as many enhancements as Wintersoft's. Certainly none that will significantly improve our efficiency."

He flipped open the brochure again, studying the charts comparing the Wintersoft program to Acton's. "After our last meeting, I did some checking, and I wondered then if ABG should switch. What I've seen today convinces me. I can't make this decision myself, obviously, but I'm meeting with the board of directors in London the week after this conference wraps up. Give me some brochures, or whatever other information you have, and I'll present a recommendation to them."

"I'd really appreciate that, Randall," Emily replied, fighting not to show her excitement. Her father would be thrilled if she managed to bring ABG over to Wintersoft. "If it would help, I can send you a complete write-up on the new software. I'll overnight it to your office as soon as I return to Boston. That way, you can peruse it before your board meeting, and if you or the other board members have any questions, you're welcome to call me. I'm happy to give you whatever information will help the board make its decision.''

Randall's smile gave Emily another shot of confidence. ''I'd like that, thanks. Oh—I almost forgot to mention—I'll be staying in Boston for three days following the London board meeting. I have to meet with some of the companies ABG finances in Massachusetts. If you're available, why don't we meet for dinner one night? I can let you know how the board meeting went, and it'll give me a chance to see the city.''

Was he asking her on a date? Or just being polite? ''I'll be in town then, so I don't see a problem. When you know your schedule, just give me a call and I'll have my secretary arrange it.''

''I'm looking forward to it.'' He nodded at Jack, then waved down a passing conference attendee—an information technology specialist from a major investment banking company, Emily noted—and merged back into the sea of people passing through the trade show.

Within seconds, Jack was at her elbow. ''Sounds like it went well. Good job.''

''I think we've got him,'' Emily couldn't help but revel in the successful pitch. ''Did you hear that last part, that he'll be bringing it up to the board of directors?''

Jack nodded, but he had the same odd look on his face he'd had at dinner the night before, when he'd implied that he should talk to Randall himself. "I heard. That's wonderful."

So what in the world did that look mean?

"Well, it sounded as though it went well with Mike Elliott," she commented, deciding it might be better not to talk about Randall Wellingby. "How about with the guy from Outland Systems? Did you talk to him about our co-marketing agreement?"

"I think we'll have everything ironed out soon. Neither of us see any major glitches."

"My father will be happy to hear that," she replied. "He wants to make sure everything's in place before the new software hits the market."

Jack assured her it would be, then abruptly turned away from her, analyzing the crowd passing by the booth. His eyes darted from face to face, and when he started talking to another potential client, his back still toward her, Emily got the impression she'd done something wrong.

What, she didn't know. But there was no way she could continue to work these shows with him for the next however-many-years if she didn't ferret it out.

For some insane reason, Jack's opinion meant too much to her.

Emily turned the pickup onto the main road from Reno to Tahoe, her foot pressing down on the accelerator harder than necessary to merge with the flow of traffic. Jack capped his pen and turned to look at her.

"Hard to take notes when you bump along like that," he said, pointing his pen at the speedometer.

"You want to drive?"

"Can't take notes that way, either."

When she didn't respond, he put away the Outland Systems folder, where he'd been jotting down a few to-do's regarding his conversation with their representative. Whatever had gotten into Emily since lunch, he didn't like it. She'd excused herself to get them sandwiches soon after talking to Randall Wellingby, but the tuna on rye hadn't improved her mood. Nor had the four diet sodas she'd sucked down that afternoon. And given her lead-footed manner now, he didn't think she'd be all that pleasant once they got back to the house.

"You did a great job today," he said, hoping to put her in a better mood.

"I suppose. For a spoiled rich girl."

Jack nearly dropped the file. Emily's tone was even, but cool. He couldn't have heard her correctly. "What?"

"I've been thinking about it all day. Last night, you seemed edgy when I told you I wanted to talk to Randall Wellingby. And then, after I had this great discussion with him, and pretty much landed ABG as a client, you get that same weird look on your face like you're about to choke."

Despite her obvious anger, her voice remained quiet and steady as she continued, "The only thing I can come up with is that you think I'm a spoiled rich girl, and that I was only promoted because my father runs the company. So no matter how well I do in this position, you're not going to give me any respect. Or trust me to land the important clients.''

''That's not true.'' Okay, it had been true for about ten minutes. When notice of her promotion first spread around the office, he'd been surprised. After all, Emily was only thirty-one. Quentin had been known as an ace in the industry, and he'd been thirty-five when he'd been promoted into the job.

But before he left, Quentin had assured Jack that Emily would be just as competent, reminding him that Lloyd never promoted anyone who didn't deserve it, and emphasizing that he'd heard great things about Emily's work ethic. And Jack had never noticed anything to counter Quentin's assertion.

In fact, he'd seen and heard quite the opposite, both around the office, as he'd started keeping tabs on her, and during this week's trip. Enough to make him immensely attracted to her, and he didn't develop crushes easily.

When Emily didn't respond, he prodded, ''What put that idea in your head? I never said anything like that.''

''You did say it. And even if you didn't, your attitude would have clued me in.''

Jack bit back a sarcastic remark. Keeping his voice calm, he asked, ''When and to whom, exactly, did I say you were a spoiled rich girl?''

''To my father. I'm surprised you don't remember.''

He relaxed against the back of the seat. ''Now I

know you're joking. Emily, if I ever said that to your father—which I wouldn't, because it's not true—Lloyd would gut me. Care to tell me what's really wrong?''

''I'm *not* joking. I was on my way into his office when I heard you say I was a 'spoiled little rich girl.' Your exact words. And then my father told you how impressed he was that you pulled yourself out of poverty—I think he said poverty, I was too distracted by the rich-girl comment to get his exact wording—and that he thought you'd go a long way with Wintersoft.''

''Okay. Now I get it.'' Jack let his head fall back against the headrest and rolled his eyes. ''I remember that conversation exactly, even if you don't. And I can tell you that you're wrong. You must have overheard from the middle, because we were talking about that airheaded woman I was unfortunate enough to have brought with me to the dinner party. I was embarrassed by her behavior and wanted to apologize to your father. That's all.''

Emily stiffened beside him. ''So you weren't talking about me?''

''No.''

She was quiet for a moment before asking, ''So since I've clearly put my foot in my mouth, what was that look about at dinner last night?''

''I don't think I had a look. If I did, that's bad. I can't negotiate favorable business deals if the other side knows what I'm thinking all the time.''

She laughed at that. ''I don't think that's a problem.

You're the type to hold your cards close to your chest.''

But her voice turned serious as she added, ''Still, I got the impression you wanted to talk to Randall Wellingby yourself—you just didn't want to come right out and tell me not to. I didn't say anything last night, because for all we knew, Randall wouldn't even be at the conference. But then, after I *did* talk to Randall, you didn't seem to agree that I'd convinced him to switch ABG to Wintersoft.''

She shifted in her seat so she could catch his eye. ''I'm right, aren't I?''

Jack exhaled as Emily turned her gaze back to the road, putting on the blinker so she could switch lanes and take the exit ramp that would lead them to the cabin.

''You're right,'' he admitted. ''But it's not because you're a spoiled rich girl.''

''Then?''

''You're new to the position is all. I'd have done the same thing with anyone attending their first trade show. We can't risk losing as important a potential client as ABG.''

The edge of her mouth jerked in skepticism. ''Despite the fact I'd already met Randall in London, and I'd already built a rapport with him?''

''Yes.'' He looked sideways at her, trying to ignore the twitching muscle along the side of her mouth. ''It's nothing against you at all, Emily. It's my job to avoid any avoidable mistakes.''

She drummed her fingers on the wheel. ''You

couldn't just tell me this? In the whole week we had the sales force putting together the materials, during any of the times we were prepping our presentation or talking to our software developers to make sure we had our facts straight—''

"We were never alone at the office. And I think it's inappropriate to tell you in front of a slew of people that, 'Hey, I'm not sure you should handle any of the really important accounts until I get a chance to see how you perform.' Don't you agree? And once we got here…I don't know. It felt wrong to say anything. I didn't want you to think I questioned your abilities. Because I don't."

"All right." She let out a long breath. "I have to say, it's the same thing my father would do in your position. No wonder he likes you so much."

Jack shrugged. Lloyd liked everyone until they proved he shouldn't. "It's not your father I'm worried about." He waited until she looked his way to continue. "It wasn't my intention to step on your toes. You're damned good at what you do."

"In that case, I'm sorry I got so ticked about it. I should have realized." They drove in silence for a few minutes, until Emily ventured, "Tell you what. I'll make it up to you with a casserole."

"Compliments of Mrs. Wilbur?"

"Hey, I'll reheat it. I'll even set the table."

Jack grinned. "So I'm forgiven?"

"For now." She rolled the truck to a stop alongside the home's security gate, and after keying in the code, pulled forward once more.

Jack waited for her to roll up her window before prodding, "What do you mean, 'for now'? You expect me to step in it again?"

"I sure hope not." She shot him a smile that made him feel better than it should have. What was it about Emily Winters? He'd never cared about Quentin's professional opinion of him half so much as he did Emily's, and it bugged him. Something about her— something more than just physical attraction—put him off-kilter whenever they were alone together.

"But I do want to know why you're so skeptical about the deal with ABG going through," she continued, unwilling to let him off the hook. "Do you think I misread Randall's excitement about the new software? Or was there something you would have done differently if you'd have been the one to speak to him?"

Her tone made it clear she thought he might be ready to offer a tip—some kind of advice on how to approach a potential client, some zinger she could deliver to get a fence-sitter to commit. Little did she know.

"Let's discuss it over casserole," he suggested. "Business talk is more palatable when you have a glass of wine in your hand, and I noticed a nice Pinot Grigio in the refrigerator." He offered her a grin he hoped would obliterate any doubts she might have about his belief in her professionalism. "If your father doesn't mind our indulgence."

"He'd probably encourage it." Her nose crinkled, and before he could ask what she meant, she clarified,

"You know, as a celebration. We did well today, don't you think?"

He nodded as she opened her car door to step out, unwilling to pursue the topic while standing in the snow. Besides, maybe she'd take what he had to say a little better with a glass of wine in hand.

Emily swirled the chilled wine in her glass as Jack took his last bite of casserole. Mrs. Wilbur's cooking always put her in a relaxed mood, and knowing the first day of the trade show was a success edged her spirits up another notch.

But then there was Jack. So she'd misinterpreted his questioning look last night. Thank goodness. But despite their easy rapport over dinner, something seemed off. He'd hardly touched his wine, despite being the one to suggest opening the bottle.

"Casserole that bad?" she teased. "I promise to lie to Mrs. Wilbur if you didn't like it."

"No, it's great." He set down his fork, but before he could turn the conversation back to food or the weather or the view—as he'd done all evening—she cut him off. "So you said we should talk about Randall Wellingby. You don't think he intends to bring ABG over to Wintersoft?"

Jack took a slow sip of his wine. "No, I'm sure he does. But I don't think it's the slam-dunk you believe."

"He approached us today, not the other way around. And he seemed very interested in what Wintersoft has to offer."

"That's the thing. I know you're going to take this the wrong way, but," he took a deep breath, "you're right. Randall approached the booth. And Randall was very interested. But he didn't approach *us*. He approached *you*. And I'm not so sure his interest was in the software."

"You have got to be kidding me." She knew she sounded indignant, but she couldn't help it. "Come on!"

"That's just what I think it was. A come-on." He held up his hand to silence her automatic protest. "Think about it. Did he or did he not ask you out to dinner?"

"By the time he comes to Boston, we may have a deal in the works. Of course he'd want to discuss it. It'd be perfectly normal for him to ask me to have dinner under those circumstances."

Jack set down his wine glass. "I don't think so. Not the way he did it. And there were things I could see that you couldn't. When you were keying up the demo, the man was definitely checking you out. He's interested."

"I think you're nuts. But hey, you're entitled to your opinion." Emily pushed away from the table and gathered their dishes, her mind silently replaying her conversation with Randall. Maybe she'd flirted with him a little, but not on purpose. She'd just been friendly, as she would be to any Wintersoft client, current or future.

She turned to put the dishes in the sink, only to see that Jack had followed her into the kitchen. "I'm sorry, Emily. I'm just not sure he's as interested in Wintersoft as he is in you.''

''I would never flirt to make a sale.''

''You didn't. That's why I didn't want to say anything. I knew you'd think I was questioning your sales skills, your integrity, or both. Truth of the matter is, you didn't do anything wrong. And *he* didn't do anything wrong, either.''

Jack set his glass in the sink alongside hers, catching her off guard when he put his hands on her shoulders and turned her to face him. ''Emily, you're a good-looking woman. Gorgeous, in fact. You're successful, and you're in line to run a profitable international software company. Men are going to be coming at you from every direction for the rest of your life. And you may not always see their true intent when your mind is focused on business.''

As if she hadn't learned that lesson with Todd. Emily exhaled, and tried not to show her nervousness— or her exhilaration—at the feel of Jack's strong hands on her shoulders. Or at his closeness, standing with his body just inches from hers in the small kitchen. No man had touched her since Todd. She couldn't exactly count Marco Valenti, since she hadn't even been attracted to him—just dated him for a while to keep her father off her back. And even if Marco had kissed her senseless, it wouldn't have compared to having Jack's warm hands on her shoulders, in a home boasting one of the most romantic views on earth.

Jack might think her mind was perpetually focused on business, but it sure wasn't now.

"If that's a compliment, which I'm guessing it is, you sure have a backhanded way of giving it," she kidded, then forced herself to twist the topic away from Jack's opinion of her. "Besides, it's awfully hard to believe what you say when you're telling me in the same breath that my judgment where Randall's concerned is off. But I'll prove to you that I'm on target with Randall. ABG will switch to Wintersoft. I'm certain."

His eyes flickered, at first in amusement, then with something else. "And I'll prove to you that *I'm* right. If not about Randall, then definitely about you."

She started to ask him to explain, but he leaned in and brushed his mouth against hers, making his meaning more than clear.

And if she found Jack Devon hard to resist before, his kiss—sweet, yet undeniably capable of becoming more—made it impossible.

Chapter Four

Jack let his hands slip from Emily's shoulders to her back. Kissing her was exactly the wrong thing to do. But months of self-imposed celibacy, combined with Emily's delicate, beautiful face looking up at him, clearly needing him to show his confidence in her, broke down his will.

Didn't the woman realize how damned perfect she was?

Just how badly had that bastard ex-husband of hers shaken her confidence, anyway?

He allowed himself to take pleasure in the feel of her full lips beneath his for just one more second, then put his hands on her waist to set her away from him. Before she could kiss him back, and before it became apparent to them both that this was more than a simple kiss of reassurance, more than something they could just brush off and still continue as business partners.

And then she kissed him back.

Pure, unfettered lust sent all thoughts of professionalism to the back of his brain as her mouth opened to his with more passion and finesse than he ever imagined. No man could stop himself now, not with a woman like Emily placing tentative hands on his waist, and certainly not at the unmistakable sound of desire that escaped her lips. She tasted of wine and warmth, of innocence and need. Their mouths fit so perfectly together—and if her hands felt like heaven through his shirt, he could only imagine...

Damn, but he wanted her in bed. And a particularly firm bed with an unspoiled view of Lake Tahoe was only steps away. At the thought of seeing Emily's long, smooth legs tangled with his, kicking aside the sheets in a moment of unstoppable need, he eased his fingers toward her throat, then under the collar of her thin white blouse.

Unable to suppress a groan at the sensation of her warm, soft skin under his fingers, he deepened their kiss, sliding his hand down until he encountered her top button. The slight resistance of the thread jerked him back to reality.

Getting in bed with any woman, let alone a coworker, and the boss's daughter, would get him fired.

And if he undid that one button, he'd undo them all. It'd take Herculean effort to stop at that point, and he'd be carrying her up the staircase within minutes.

Forcing himself to picture his office, and all he'd

worked so hard to achieve, he took a long, deep breath, then stepped back and gave her a lopsided grin he hoped appeared casual.

"There. Now are you convinced? You're attractive. And if *I* can kiss you like that, think about what's going through Randall Wellingby's mind."

Her eyes widened, and he intentionally kept his gaze off her lips, which were now tantalizingly pink. He wanted to ask her to come upstairs with him, but instead said, "Don't underestimate him. He has ulterior motives where you're concerned."

"Tell me," her voice had a raspy edge to it, just enough to let him know he'd gotten to her as much as she'd gotten to him. "Is this how you and Quentin Kostador handled your business disagreements?"

"I never had to convince Quentin he was attractive." Jack laughed, thankful she'd given him the easy out.

"Good thing, or he'd have slugged you."

"I'm surprised you didn't."

Now it was her turn to laugh. "Can't. Need you for the trade show tomorrow."

"Which we should talk about." He leaned a hip against the counter, knowing he couldn't possibly look as casual as he hoped. Not after a kiss like that. "I just need to know that you trust my instincts. If Randall swings by the booth again tomorrow, maybe I should talk to him. Then we know he'll actually be paying attention to the software."

Emily sucked in her bottom lip, but still grinned. "All right. I trust you." She turned to the sink and started to rinse off the dishes, but glanced sideways at him as she opened the dishwasher. "You know, I never thanked you last month for sticking up for me with Todd—when we caught him red-handed breaking into my computer files so he could send the information to Acton, and he tried to defend himself by spewing all that nasty stuff about me."

"Todd's a bully. And he said things to you that no one should say to another human being. You didn't deserve it." He'd forgotten all about the episode. And he hadn't stuck up for her, really—no more than she'd done herself. He took a glass from her and placed it in the top rack of the dishwasher. "I'd have done the same thing for Quentin."

"I just bet." She whacked him with a dishtowel, and his admiration for her jumped another peg. How she could play off the intense sexual heat their kiss created was beyond him. It took every ounce of his effort. "But seriously, Jack, I do trust your judgment. You're a natural at reading people, and you suspected Todd wasn't up to any good when he came by Wintersoft last month, moaning and groaning about being laid off at his new company. I missed his motives entirely, and I was married to the guy. I should have been the first person to suspect him."

"You can't make every call," he replied as they finished loading the dishes and, thankfully, made their way out of the tight confines of the galley kitchen. When they stepped down into the sunken living room, he continued, "I realized today that you get them right more than most people. Especially for being so new in your position. I wouldn't have had such a good conversation with Mike Elliott if you hadn't clued me in to the fact that Metrogroup only called our help line twice last year. Or that it's his birthday tomorrow. That was a stroke of genius.''

His gaze flicked to the piano and the family photos there. ''Must have been that Harvard education of yours,'' he teased, pointing out a picture of her standing beside her father, wearing her cap and gown.

''Don't look at that,'' she groaned. ''It was the end of the big hair era, and I didn't have the sense to abandon the style when I should have.'' She flipped the picture around, just to make her point, then sat down on the leather sofa and gestured toward one of the chairs.

Across the coffee table, he noted, where no touching could occur. Good.

After grabbing her briefcase from where she'd dropped it beside the sofa, she flipped open the file on Metrogroup. ''Okay, you already talked to Mike Elliott. I think I saw Ethan Poston's name on the list of conference attendees—he also has a lot of pull when it comes to their software decisions. Might be good if we can grab him tomorrow, just to make sure that he and Mike are getting the same message about Wintersoft.''

''Agreed,'' Jack replied, glad they were back into familiar territory. Far, far better to be talking business. Still, his eyes kept drifting to her blouse and that top button. What if he *had* opened it? What would they be doing right now? And where? Would he have carried her up to bed? Or wouldn't they have made it that far? After all, the leather sofas were only steps from the kitchen, and the fireplace was...

He caught himself as something she said popped out at him. "Sorry, what was that?" he asked, a knot of dread forming in the pit of his stomach. "I guess my mind was still on my discussion with Mike."

A little line appeared between her eyes. "I was just saying that perhaps you should talk to Ethan Poston. I'd be more than happy to if you're occupied with another potential client, of course, but according to my notes, he's an Amherst grad. Went on scholarship. Since you went to Amherst, and on scholarship, no less, it'll give you a connection you could work from."

The knot in his stomach suddenly turned to a cold, wrenching fist. "How'd you know I went to Amherst?"

She shrugged, but didn't meet his gaze. "I think I've always known. Anyway, I think you should talk with Ethan, if we get the chance, since—"

"I never told you I went to Amherst. I don't have my diploma in my office, either. And I certainly never said I went on scholarship."

"Then I'm sure Carmella must have told me at some point. She knows everything about everyone, you know." The same wary look flickered in her eyes he'd seen earlier, when Lloyd had first told them they'd be staying at the house in Tahoe together instead of in separate hotel rooms in Reno.

"I never told Carmella." He leaned forward, dropping the file to the glass-topped coffee table. "Emily, you read my personnel file, didn't you?"

In an instant, he knew. Just from the look on her face, though he doubted anyone else could have guessed at her internal panic. One thing he'd learned from his father—how to analyze a competitor's "tells"—the little facial tics or nervous movements that give away the fact they have an ace in the hole. Or that they're bluffing. As Emily said, his ability to read people made him good at his job. Even if it made him curse himself at this moment.

"You did," he shook his head, his voice betraying his anger—or his disappointment—to her. "The last time I went to Human Resources, though, the department secretary couldn't locate it. My file and five others were misplaced, and she found that odd, since so few people have access to them. I am very careful about my personal information. I went to update my phone number twice this year, so I knew someone had been in there recently. I thought it might have been Todd Baxter, since we know he illegally accessed the files on the beta version of our new software suite. I couldn't fathom why he'd be in the personnel files, though, especially given that he was trying to get information that might interest Acton, but then again, he wasn't in the personnel files, was he?"

Emily bit her lip. "I'm sorry, Jack. You're right. But it's not what you think."

"You weren't just in mine. There were six files misplaced—all members of Wintersoft's senior staff.

You were in my file, Matt Burke's, Grant Lawson's, Brett Hamilton's, Reed Connors's, and Nate Leeman's. Those were the files the secretary couldn't locate.'' He ticked them off on his fingers as he went. "Nate's was what made me suspect it might be Todd snooping around. After all, Nate's the Senior Vice President of Technology. But the others didn't make sense.

He pushed out of the leather seat and strode to the window. He couldn't stand seeing the guilty look on her face, any more than he could let her actions slide. He had to know.

Spinning around, he had to force himself not to shout, "Why?"

"I can't tell you."

"The hell you can! It's my private information. My life."

She blanched, but remained still. "I know it. And it was wrong for me to be in your files."

He remained silent, and for the first time, he saw fear in her eyes. "I'll tell you what I can, but you have to make me a promise first."

"Uh-uh," he shook his head. "No promises."

She stood and crossed her arms over her chest, defiant. Where she got off being so self-righteous, he couldn't imagine. After all, she was the one caught with her fingers in the files, not him.

"What do you think of Carmella Lopez?" she demanded.

"Love her to death. Doesn't everyone?"

"And what do you think of my father?"

"I owe him my livelihood. He taught me everything I know." Almost. His own father taught him the most bitter lessons of life, but then, only by example. *Bad* example. Lloyd had been more a father to him—in the true sense of the word—than his own had ever been.

"Then if I tell you what I can, you need to promise not to be angry with Carmella. Or to go to my father with this."

He pulled in a deep breath. "I promise not to be mad at Carmella. But I reserve the right to be mad at you, and I reserve the right to go to your father if I think it's in the best interest of the company. I owe my allegiance to him, not to you."

"Fine." She uncrossed her arms, though her eyes remained wary. "Carmella and I both accessed the files. She's legally entitled, and I am, too, so technically we didn't do anything wrong. We were working on a project—something very important. If I could explain, you'd understand why I had to do it."

"But you can't."

She gave her head a slight shake no. "To do so might hurt my father, both personally and professionally. And it would breach the privacy of the other men whose files I accessed."

He let out a snort. "That makes no sense at all."

"I know. But that's all I can say."

He tilted his head back and stared at the ceiling for a moment. He couldn't imagine Emily and Carmella reading through his files for any underhanded purposes. And he had to admit, he was relieved it was them, and not Todd Baxter. Not that there was any incriminating information about his father in his personnel file, but Todd couldn't be trusted. Carmella could. And despite what she'd done, he knew in his gut that Emily could be, too.

He turned his gaze back to Emily. "I don't want you in my files ever again. For any purpose. Not without coming to me first. I have a right to know who's in there and why."

"No worries there. The reason I accessed them doesn't exist any longer."

"It's the same with the other files?"

"Definitely not going in those again. I can't tell you any more. I'm sorry." She swallowed, then gestured to the files on the coffee table. "Listen, we have to look these over, and fast. My father's due to call us in less than half an hour, and as well as you seem to be able to read my mind, he's better. The last thing we want is for him to think we're not getting along swimmingly. Or for him to worry that the trade show's not going as well as he'd hoped. Right?"

Jack swore under his breath, but agreed. "All right. Let's focus on getting prepped for tomorrow."

Relief washed over her face. "Thanks."

He took his seat, then flipped open the Metrogroup file again. As she reached across the coffee table for the file on ABG, he caught her wrist. "We're not done talking about this, Emily. Sooner or later, I want to know why you accessed those files. That's a promise I *can* make."

*   *   *

How could she make two monster-size mistakes in just one hour? Emily swirled her coffee, took a sip, then inspected the software brochures set along the front table of the Wintersoft booth to ensure they were within easy reach of conference-goers. She had a feeling this wouldn't be her only coffee of the day, given how poorly she'd slept after what had happened last night.

At least the call from her father had gone well. She'd taken Jack's advice and downplayed Randall's interest in the software, assuring her father they'd continue to pursue ABG. Lloyd's excitement over keeping Metrogroup as a client and Jack's impending deal with Outland Systems were obvious, just from the tone of his voice.

But then her father asked how they were enjoying the house. While Jack might not have caught the underlying question in her father's voice, it had been evident to Emily. But Jack, smooth as ever, complimented Lloyd on the home's architecture and thanked him for arranging to have the kitchen stocked with such delicious food.

Her father hadn't noticed that Jack neglected to mention her, but the chill she'd felt coming from Jack's direction during the call was unmistakable.

How could she have let it happen? After months of keeping the matchmaking plan quiet, of being cautious not to let the slightest hint drop, she'd slipped up with Jack Devon, of all people. If he did decide to broach the subject with Carmella—or her father— they'd be humiliated.

She turned away from the Wintersoft brochures and took a long gulp of her coffee, ignoring the burn in her throat. Well, better that Jack dislike her than kiss her. Her other colossal mistake.

Jack's back bumped against hers, jostling her coffee as he shifted the computer display on the table so passersby could get a better view.

"Sorry," he muttered, not bothering to turn around.

"S'okay." She wouldn't bother with him, either. That mind-blowing kiss happened the last time she bothered, and she wasn't about to do *that* again.

As much as Jack tried to play off what happened, tried to pretend it hadn't meant anything, she knew better. No one kissed like that just to prove a business point, not even a sex god like Jack Devon. How lame an excuse was that?

He obviously knew what she did—that despite their apparent mutual attraction, a relationship between them was impossible. He'd seen what happened with Todd. Dating her could mean losing his job.

As depressed as that thought made her, she was as willing to grab at an excuse for the kiss as he was.

Fortunately, the exhibition hall opened its doors, and Mike Elliott and Ethan Poston of Metrogroup entered at the front of the line. As planned, Jack quickly roped in Ethan, giving him the full demonstration of the upgraded software. A member of the exhibition hall staff approached Emily with a quick question, and for the rest of the morning, she didn't have to think about Jack.

By lunchtime, however, the hall began to clear out. After Emily thanked a client for stopping by to say hello, she realized Jack was standing behind her, waiting until she was finished.

Reluctantly, she turned to him. "Morning go well?"

He nodded. "I think Ethan's on board. Keeping Metrogroup shouldn't be a concern. And I had the chance to talk to the team from one of the investment banking companies, too."

"I saw that." Emily looked around the hall, surprised to see that only a few conference attendees remained, but more surprised to see Acton and others packing up their booths. Keeping her hand below the table, so the people from Acton couldn't see, she gestured toward their exhibit. "What's with that?"

"AGM's this afternoon. Remember? Trade show's done for the day."

How could she forget? Of course the association wanted all the conference attendees to attend their Annual General Meeting, which meant trade-show booths were expected to close for the day, out of courtesy.

"So, I guess we're closing up shop." She eyed their dwindling stack of brochures, and realized that Jack had already shut off the computers and locked them down. "Closing up shop" wouldn't take long, and then she'd be stuck at the house with Jack for the entire afternoon.

"Yep." His face showed the same hesitation she

felt. He apparently didn't care to be alone with her, either.

"Well, we only have one vehicle here in Reno, so we're sort of stuck coming and going together. You can always get my dad's sedan out of the garage and go off on your own if you like. I'm sure he wouldn't mind." When Jack looked less than excited about driving around Tahoe alone all afternoon, she ventured, "Since we don't have much to work on, why don't we go gambling? The Silver Legacy and the El Dorado are just across the street. And it's not a long walk to Harrah's, either." He could sit at his slot machine, she could sit at hers, and never a word of conversation had to pass between them.

He didn't answer immediately, so she prodded, "I have my dad's frequent player card in my purse. You're welcome to use it. Maybe you'll get a chance to stand in the booth at the Silver Legacy when they do the grab for dollars. You ever seen it? You'd get a kick out of it."

Jack's expression turned to astonishment. "You— and your *father*—have frequent player cards? You both gamble?"

"Sure," she shrugged. "We spend as much time in Nevada as possible. Only makes sense to chalk up playing credits for dinner coupons and free hotel stays. I think my dad gave our last free hotel stay to Carmella. She came with one of her girlfriends and had a wonderful time."

As soon as Carmella's name passed her lips, she knew she'd stepped in it again, reminding Jack of the fact she and Carmella had accessed his personal information.

Instead of mentioning the files, however, Jack picked up the brochures and stuffed them into one of the boxes beneath the exhibition table. "I'd prefer not to gamble, if that's all right with you. But I'm not too keen on sitting in the house or driving your dad's sedan all over creation, either."

He straightened, then met her gaze and raised an eyebrow. "You ski?"

"Of course."

"Ethan Poston mentioned that he skipped part of the conference yesterday to ski. Said the snow was great, and it's not too cold. Maybe we can rent some equipment and get a half-day pass to Heavenly."

Emily's spirits instantly lifted. Skiing would be perfect. Fun, but no conversation expected. "Heavenly would be a blast—but if you want to get on the slopes faster, we should go to Diamond Peak. It's closer to the house and less crowded. Plus, the views are spectacular. But I'm open to anything." Anything that would keep her from being alone with Jack. On a ski slope filled with the first wave of college kids on spring break, there wasn't much risk of repeating their kitchen mistake.

"You're the semi-local. I'll go wherever you suggest." He pushed the box of brochures under the table, then grabbed a bottle of water. "I'll have to rent equipment."

"True. Shouldn't be a problem, though." She had

a thought, then glanced down at his feet. They looked about right. "What size shoe do you wear?"

"Twelve."

"So does my father. You're welcome to try his skis and boots. If they fit, it'll save us time."

Jack shot her a sideways glance as they walked toward the exit. "Sure he wouldn't mind? Most people are pretty picky about lending out their ski equipment."

"Not my father." *And definitely not with you.*

"Just wait until I leave a three-inch scratch across the top of one of his skis. He'll change his mind."

Emily bit her lip to keep from laughing out loud. Jack could destroy her father's skis for all Lloyd would care if it meant Jack would be spending time with his daughter. But in Emily's mind, a day on the slopes sure beat hanging around the house. Not only would the adrenaline rush distract Jack from the fact she'd been digging around in his files, it would give them something to talk about besides business for the remainder of their time together in Nevada. She could easily wax poetic about ski runs and snow conditions for a few more days.

At least she hoped so.

Chapter Five

Within seconds of snapping his booted feet into the bindings of Lloyd Winters's top-of-the-line Rossignols, Jack knew they'd made the right decision. A few quick runs would clear his mind and allow him to work off his agitation. Working side-by-side with Emily in the booth all day had only fueled it.

It galled him, her request that he not get mad, especially after what happened in the kitchen. How could he not be irate at such an invasion of his privacy? Had she just been Emily, and not Emily, daughter-of-the-boss, type-of-girl-who-wants-a-commitment, and therefore everything he'd sworn not to allow himself, he might've even taken her to bed. Or at least let things continue in that direction. And wouldn't *that* have been a mistake?

Still, he had to admit a grudging respect that Emily

had asked on behalf of Carmella, and knew better than to ask he not be angry with her.

He let out a huff of air, then zipped the last few inches of his ski jacket to cover his throat.

His anger would abate with time. He wasn't the type to hold grudges, and besides, Emily hadn't learned anything that might tip her off to his secret. She apparently had no clue. He waited while Emily interlaced her fingers, pushing her gloves on until they were snug. Instinct said she hadn't read through the files for a malicious reason. Emily wasn't the malicious type—quite the opposite. She'd been the one to help out the company's public relations manager, Ariana Fitzpatrick—now Ariana Lawson—when Ariana was pregnant with twins. Emily had also quietly taken on extra duties so Brett Hamilton, the VP of Wintersoft's Overseas Division, could take a longer honeymoon with his new wife, Sunny.

And he was pretty certain Emily had something to do with the company's VP of Global Marketing, Reed Connors, finding his son a couple of months before. If that didn't qualify her for angel status, he wasn't sure what would.

So if she wasn't suspicious about his background, what did she hope to learn from his file? He skied ahead of Emily toward the bottom of the lift, turning over every possibility in his mind, but couldn't make sense of it. Why couldn't she simply ask the employees involved whatever it was she needed to know? And how long had her snooping been going on?

It had to be something all six men had in common.

What, other than the fact they were all upper-level management at Wintersoft, he couldn't fathom.

"How much of a warm-up do you need?" Emily asked, shuffling forward in the chairlift line so they stood shoulder-to-shoulder. An infectious smile tugged at the edges of her lips as she looked at the lift, then toward the trees and the peaks beyond. He'd never have pictured her as the outdoorsy type, but the cool mountain air gave her cheeks a rosy cast that suited her complexion perfectly. Of course, he'd only seen her color that way once before—right after he'd kissed her.

He shrugged, trying to keep his mind on the files. Things would be easier if he could focus on all the reasons he had to dislike her. "Not much. Besides, we only have a few hours until dark."

"True." Emily pointed toward the lift with one pole. "This is the Lodgepole Quad. If you want to start out easy, we can do a quick run from the top of this lift back here to the base, then take it up again and continue on to the Crystal Quad. That's how you get to the intermediate slopes." A playful grin spread over her face, making her more beautiful, if that was possible. "The Crystal Quad also leads to the expert slopes. But we don't have to do those at all, if you don't want."

"Well, if you'd prefer not to—"

"I'm flexible. I'll ski wherever."

"Me, too." He couldn't stop one side of his mouth from lifting in a barely concealed smile at her competitive spirit. "So after one easy run, let's go for the tough stuff."

Amusement lit her gaze as they advanced to the front of the line. "You've got it."

They shuffled into position, then sat back in the wide chair as the lift came around to carry them up the mountain. Jack closed his eyes as soon as they were airborne, allowing the brisk air to fill his lungs and push away the stress of the day. How long had it been since he'd allowed himself a vacation? Too long. He hoped his skills hadn't deteriorated.

He hazarded a glance at Emily. They had plenty of space between them, since the chair usually carried four people, so she'd twisted sideways in the seat, watching over the side of the chair while skiers glided down the slope below.

Why did she have to be so beautiful? The lift afforded them a stunning view of the slope, but his eyes stayed riveted on Emily. A pair of goggles rested atop her head, and she'd pulled her hair into a long brown braid, which hung down past her shoulders. He'd never seen her wearing casual clothes. Even at the house, she didn't change into jeans or sweats, but kept on her business clothes until disappearing into her room at night. Both mornings, she'd come down to breakfast ready to go—hair done, skirt straight, suit jacket over her arm.

This outing afforded him an entirely different vision of her.

It hadn't taken her long to get ready once they'd returned to the house after the trade show. He wondered if it was because she skied frequently enough to whip the proper clothing out of her closet without having to think about it, or because she couldn't wait to get out of the house and avoid spending any more time than necessary cooped up alone with him.

Judging from the quality of her ski equipment and ease at handling it, together with the amount of time she'd spent around Tahoe, he had to assume her skiing abilities were well-honed. But the tension between them—from both the kiss and the blowup that followed—made him assume her speed had more to do with him than with the rapidly setting sun.

He turned away from her and studied the layout of the ski runs below them. Whatever her reason for wanting to get on the mountain as quickly as possible, no way was he going to let Emily Winters clean his clock on the way down.

"Did you ski much growing up?"

He heard the rustle of her ski jacket against the cool metal chair as she turned to face him, but he kept his gaze trained on the slope below. "Not really. Picked it up as an adult." Even if he'd wanted to, he couldn't have afforded it as a kid growing up in the shadow of the Quincy Shipyards. Skiing, like golf and tennis, was considered a rich kids' sport. The one time his mother had scrounged the fee for him to go on a ski trip in central Massachusetts with his church group, his father found another use for the money. As usual.

"Did your parents ski?"

"Nah." He wished. Maybe a different hobby

would have kept his father on the straight and narrow, and given his parents something in common again. Something to laugh about and to document in family photos, as Emily's family had done.

Needing to change the subject, he pointed out a skier about to run through a patch of moguls. "Look at that guy. Not bad."

Emily laughed, then lifted the tips of her skis. "Better to keep your eyes forward. We're almost to the top."

As soon as their skis hit the snow, Emily veered off to the right, to the top of the run. Despite his vow to concentrate on the files, and not on his attraction to her, his stomach clenched with desire as she turned and winked at him, then slipped her goggles over her eyes and took off down the slope.

He managed to catch her near the top, but lost her again as she weaved back and forth across the snow, then crouched low and bombed the bottom third of the run. He tucked in behind her, his skis fitting neatly into the tracks left by hers. As he grew accustomed to the feel of his weight over the skis and the bite of cold air against his face, he glanced forward, and caught sight of her rear, only inches off the ground as she crouched above her skis.

Oh, yes, skiing would *definitely* work off his anger. And replace it with something even more unwelcome.

She slid into the lift line just ahead of him, her face glowing with the effort of the run. "Well, ready to do one of the tougher slopes?"

"Fine by me." Now that he had the requisite adrenaline rush.

The line moved quickly, and before Jack had time to think, he and Emily were being carried skyward once more, their skis hanging in the air below them as the lift took them up the slope. This time, instead of awkward conversation, laughter filled the time. Once off the lift, they skied a short distance to another lift, one that would carry them to the top of Diamond Peak.

"Get ready. You're about to get the best view in all of Nevada," Emily promised.

"Better than at the house?"

"Doesn't even compare."

A few minutes later, when they reached the summit, he let out an amazed, "Wow."

Beside him, Emily shoved her goggles back to the top of her head so she could get an unobstructed view. Lake Tahoe stretched out below them, surrounded by mountains covered in snow-dusted evergreens. The afternoon sun glinted off the clear blue surface of the lake, sending flashes of light in every direction.

In all his life, he'd never seen water so blue and clear.

"Beautiful, isn't it?" She shot him a disarming grin. "Now aren't you glad we had the afternoon off?"

A laugh escaped him at her tone, which made it obvious she'd had the same concerns about spending the afternoon off with him as he'd had with her.

Her acknowledgement of their tension had the surprising effect of making him feel even more comfortable with her. Too comfortable, just as he had felt after she'd allowed him to play off their kiss with a joke.

How did she get under his skin so easily?

He returned her smile, then looked back toward the water. "This isn't the best view in Nevada. It has to be one of the best in the world."

"I agree, but I'm biased. I took it down a notch by saying Nevada. Didn't want to oversell it."

"Well, you sure know how to sell a product." Against his better judgment, he reached over, putting a hand on her arm. "And I've known it all along. For months, if not years. I shouldn't have questioned your ability to carry off the deal with Randall Wellingby and ABG."

"You said it yourself, you'd do the same for anyone new to my position."

"I should have known better with you. It wasn't warranted. Forgive me?"

"Only if you'll—" She waved one black-gloved hand, cutting off her own comment. "I forgive you. Already forgave you."

"Em," he squeezed her arm. "You're forgiven, too. I won't ask about the files again."

Before she could speak, he used one of his poles to knock the excess snow from one of his boots, then snapped it back into its binding and winked. "Now, see if you'll forgive me for out-skiing you. Bet I beat you to the bottom this time."

"Oh, no you don't!"

But before she could flip her goggles back into place, he pushed off, following the signs to the Crystal Ridge run. She soon passed him, but he cut around a mogul to take the lead again. He reveled in the feeling of the snow blowing up into his face as he sliced from one side of the slope to the other, dodging around Emily, who appeared to be enjoying herself as much as he was.

Catching her attention, he angled his skis toward the black diamond sign for the Diamond Back run. He allowed her to pull ahead of him, holding her body in a tight tuck as she rounded the corner to the difficult slope just ahead of him. Within seconds, she straightened, keeping her upper body squared as her lower body negotiated a series of moguls with the skill of a pro. She came to a stop at an open space, and he turned to a stop just above her, spraying her with snow and ice.

"Very funny," she laughed, her breath coming in puffs from the effort of skiing through the moguls.

"Had to make you earn that apology," he teased. "And besides, it's obvious to me who's the better skier."

"Hey—"

"I'm faster, but you're more skilled. So I have to take my chances to spray you when they come—I have a feeling you'll get me back."

"You're on." With the tip of her pole, she pointed to a spot about fifty yards below them, across the run. "See that gap between the evergreens? There's a trail through the trees that connects this run to Battle Born.''

"The bunny hill, right?"

She snorted. "I think not."

He gave her a half-bow and used his pole to gesture toward the trail. "After you, milady."

She kicked her skis around so they aimed for the trees, then took off ahead of him.

As he backhanded loose snow off his jacket, he grinned to himself. *This* was how things should be between them. Relaxed, fun. Teasing, but not too intimate.

Safe.

He pushed off, and spying the flash of Emily's light blue ski jacket nearing the trees, he crossed the run to catch her.

She turned, ducking in anticipation of entering the forest. At the same moment her attention focused on the trail, a bright yellow blur cut across the slope above her, then directly into Emily's path.

"Em!" he yelled, knowing he couldn't stop the snowboarder from hitting her.

At the last second, the boarder saw Emily and made a hard turn back to the center of the ski run. Emily dodged at the same time, but lost control. Leaning to the side, one pole behind her, and with only one ski on the ground, she headed onto the narrow, wooded trail, then out of Jack's sight.

Panic ripped through Emily as she managed to dodge one tree, only to be smacked in the face by the needles of another, knocking her farther off balance. She couldn't avoid a crash—the question was, how bad would it be? Stupid snowboarder. How could that kid not have seen her?

Finally, the one ski she still had in contact with the ground slipped, and she went careening off the path, headfirst, then rear first, into the trees. The thinned-out underbrush scraped at her cheeks until she managed to bring herself to a stop between two snow-laden evergreens, both of which promptly rained a shower of needles and ice onto her head.

She laughed to herself in relief as she swiped the snow from her face. Thank goodness, a soft landing. Still, Jack had to be eating this up.

She flopped onto her back to catch her breath, spent from the effort of keeping herself from going head-to-tree-trunk. Now she'd have to hike back up the hill on one ski to retrieve the other—it had popped off somewhere in the brush above her when she fell.

"Emily!" Jack's voice rang through the evergreens. From the rustling above her, he'd pulled off the path and was headed down to her. She hoped he'd seen her ski and thought to pick it up.

She opened her mouth to answer, but he came crashing into the snow beside her, sending another coating of icy powder over her in his rush to help.

"Emily, are you all right?"

"What's with spraying me twice in a row?" She turned toward him, then reluctantly pushed up on one elbow. "Is this your way of gloating?"

"I thought for sure you—"

"A little scratched, but no big deal." She couldn't help but offer him a comforting smile in an effort to relieve the worry furrowing his brow. All morning, she'd felt anger rolling off him in waves, and could hardly wait to get away from the trade-show floor. Now, those hours seemed as if they'd happened weeks before. Even with her wreck, hitting the slopes—getting away from the stress of work—had been a perfect idea. Just the thing to ease the hostility between them.

He pulled off one of his gloves, then reached out to touch her cheek, his fingers gentle as they turned her face toward his. "You don't look all right. You're bleeding over here, in front of your ear. Must've caught a tree branch on the way down."

"Just a scratch." She'd had enough of them over the years she could tell without removing her gloves to feel the injury herself. "I'm more embarrassed than hurt."

The concern in his dark gaze melted her heart, and she hoped he couldn't see her reaction on her face. "I was supposed to be dazzling you with my expert skiing abilities. Now I'll be explaining away scrapes at the trade show."

His fingers stilled on her face, and his voice dropped to a low rumble. "You're dazzling as you are."

"The snow is blinding you. Are *you* all right?" He'd genuinely feared for her.

Just as she registered that he was going to kiss her, a group of teenagers cut through the trees on the trail above them, whooping as they went. Jarred back to reality, Jack turned toward the sound.

"Guess we should get up," Emily said, pushing herself to her feet and away from Jack. She looked around, trying to locate her missing ski in an effort to hide her jumpiness over the near-kiss. "You didn't happen to get my other—"

"Pushed it in front of me." He rolled to grab the ski from where it was embedded in the powder behind him, then shoved it along the surface of the snow so she could snap her boot back into the binding.

As soon as he was upright, they climbed back up to the trail. "On to Battle Born?" she asked.

"If you're still up for it." Skepticism tinged his voice.

"Sure. The fall wasn't anything. Really." She gestured down the trail to where it opened onto the wide slope in front of them. "Can't avoid it at this point, anyway. Only way down to the lift."

They skied without incident the rest of the afternoon, stopping to take in the sight of the lake from different areas, laughing as they followed each other's ski trails down the mountain. But the playful, easy spirit that colored their first two runs never returned, and Emily knew it was because of the kiss-that-wasn't.

Chapter Six

By the time the sun began to dip below the mountains and the lights of the base lodge glowed against the white snow, visible even from high on the slopes, Emily was ready to call it a day, despite the fact they'd be forced to dodge their all-too-apparent mutual attraction in the tight confines of the house. Jack must've felt as exhausted as she did, because after looking over his shoulder to catch her attention, he pointed past the line for the lift and indicated he wanted to head for the lodge instead.

"Fine," she yelled.

He waited for her beside the ski rack, and wordlessly, they headed for the rest rooms, then bought bottles of water from the concession stand and started stripping off their gear on a nearby bench.

"How'd those work?" Emily asked, nodding toward Jack's borrowed boots and ski pants. The pants were a little tighter on him than on her father—Jack had a lot more muscle to his physique than her father—but she wasn't about to complain.

"Great. But I noticed you're limping."

"Just adjusting from walking in ski boots to wearing shoes again."

"Or that fall took more out of you than you care to admit."

She snorted. Her ankle started bugging her on the last two runs, but she'd shake it off by morning. Certainly it wasn't so bad he'd noticed? "Now I know you're a natural for business development. Always looking for the angle to make yourself look stronger than the competition."

He raised an eyebrow. "You're not the competition."

"Jack—"

"You've had a rough afternoon. Let me get you back to the house and get you some hot chocolate. You need to put your feet up so that ankle won't swell. And I won't even remind you that I beat you down that last run."

How could he be so sweet? Chivalrous and affable, yet never revealing anything about himself. It drove her nuts at the same time it fueled her entirely inappropriate lust.

"Unless you needed to spend the evening reviewing the Goldman Sachs files," he prodded. "I could coach you on how to approach their representative—"

"Very funny. Let's pick up a pizza and a video in

Incline Village on the way." A good movie would keep them from having to talk. Or think about what was happening between them.

"Done."

An hour later, Jack located paper plates and napkins in the kitchen, while Emily filled two glasses with soda and carried them to the coffee table, nestled between the leather sofa and chairs. With a click of the remote, a panel opened in the cherry cabinetry opposite the fireplace to reveal a wide-screen television. She turned to pick up the video, an action flick Jack had picked up—she'd intentionally kept him far from the wall of Meg Ryan and Sandra Bullock romantic comedies—but as she leaned forward, her ankle buckled under her, nearly sending her to the floor.

"I knew you were hurt worse than you said." Jack caught her under her arms, then eased her to the sofa. How had he gotten to the living room so quickly? "Your ankle?"

"It's nothing, just took a misstep." She gave him a smile of reassurance. "But thanks for catching me."

Jack's forehead creased in doubt. He studied her for a moment, then pushed the napkins and soda glasses aside.

"What are you doing?"

"What you won't. Taking care of you." Before she could protest, he had his hands around her calf, lifting her foot to rest on the coffee table, all the time handling her as if she might break.

"Jack, I'm fine—"

He slid a throw pillow under her foot, then knelt

to the floor, removed her sock, and pushed up the leg of her pants toward her knee.

"Jack!"

He ignored her as he ran his fingers over her elevated ankle, checking for injury. Finding nothing obvious, he met her gaze and frowned, his steel-gray eyes serious. "Why do you work so hard to appear invincible? You're not. No one is. But you can't let anyone see even a glimpse of vulnerability in you. Can you?"

If only he knew how vulnerable she felt at that very moment. She steered her thoughts away from his firm, sensuous fingers, which now rested on her bare leg, just below where he'd rolled up her pants.

"Maybe because I'm not hurt."

"Liar."

"My ankle's fine. Just a little sore. Believe me, I've been injured enough times while skiing to know if something's worth worrying over. By tomorrow I'll have forgotten all about it."

"I wasn't talking about your ankle." Could the man read minds? She reached next to her on the sofa for the video box, anxious to get the movie started and to get the conversation off her.

He let go of her leg and eased onto the sofa beside her. "Is it because your father runs Wintersoft? You're afraid of how everyone else in the company will perceive you, that they'll think you didn't get your job on your own merits?"

She leaned her head back against the sofa cushions

and stared up at the ceiling. "You're determined to psychoanalyze me, aren't you?"

"Humor me. We still have three days here, and it'd be a lot more comfortable if we could drop the charades."

She straightened and looked him in the eye. How could she not? "In that case, you're right. At least partially. Wouldn't you work a little harder if your father ran the company? If your performance reflected on him?"

He turned, his arm coming to rest on the sofa just behind her shoulders. "I'm sure I would. But it's more than that. You don't even let your guard down when it's just you and your father. He's the most generous man I've met in my life, yet you of all people seem uncomfortable with him. I've seen you together around the office enough to know. Why?"

"If I told you that it has to do with the files, and that I can't talk about it, will you drop it?"

"What do you think?"

Man, he was a pest. But the concern in his eyes made her believe he wasn't thinking of himself—or the files.

"You promised not to ask about the files any—"

"Em, just tell me already. You have to know by now I wouldn't do anything to hurt your father, no matter what. Or you." His voice was low, reassuring. And turning her on, dammit. Did he know he had this effect on her?

She leaned back, unwilling to meet his gaze directly, but brushed up against his arm. He shifted, allowing it to fall across her shoulders.

How could such a simple touch fog her brain? She swallowed hard, trying to focus. "You were with the company during my marriage to Todd. You know how miserably that turned out."

"You didn't advertise your feelings. But divorce can't be easy, even when it's the right thing to do."

She looked at him in surprise. "Are you speaking from experience?"

"My parents *should* have divorced, let's leave it at that. Just as you were right to divorce Todd Baxter. Last month, when Todd was caught stealing secrets, I have to admit, I wondered how such a rotten human being ever had the fortune to marry someone like you."

She snorted. "My father, that's how."

"Come again?"

What was it that made her want to tell him, Mr. Secrets himself? Yet despite all logic, everything that said it was the last thing she should share with a co-worker, especially a co-worker who'd kissed her, she knew it'd be the right thing to do.

"My father loves me very much." She took care in choosing her words. "But as much as he loves me, he's always wanted a son more. Someone with the Winters name who could head up the company after he died. But my parents had fertility problems. They were fortunate just to have me."

Jack shook his head. "I find that hard to believe. The part about your dad wanting a son, that is."

"He's never said it in so many words, but..." she shrugged. "Sometimes kids can tell things about their parents, you know? Having a son was my dad's dream, the one thing that would've made him feel complete."

Jack gave her a slow nod, and she could see he understood.

"Well, when Todd Baxter started at the company, the same year I graduated from college, my father saw him as this golden boy. A good-looking guy only a couple years older than his daughter. Someone ambitious, with a good education."

"The son he never had?"

"Exactly. I thought Todd was good-looking and nice enough, and he came from a good family. He was intelligent enough to impress my father. All the usual qualifications for someone you'd want to date. So when my father encouraged me to go out with Todd, I did. Eventually, we got married."

She sighed, trying not to fiddle with the trim on the edge of the leather sofa, or to think too much about the feel of Jack's strong, comforting arm across her shoulders. "It seemed like the next logical step in life, I suppose. I was twenty-three when we got engaged, twenty-four when we married. I had just received my first promotion, landing a great job in the sales department, and all my friends were getting married.'' She screwed up her mouth. "But I knew, almost from the first, that it wasn't right.''

He reached over with his free arm to hold her hand, caressing the backs of her fingers. Rather than shy away from the touch, though, she interlaced her fingers with his on top of her propped leg.

"You stuck it out a long time.'' His voice barely topped a whisper.

"Eighteen months. Toughest eighteen months of my life. But I didn't want to let my father down. And I didn't want to admit to myself what a horrible mistake I'd made.''

"Todd must have known how you felt.''

"I'm not sure. I don't think he ever really understood me. Still, I tried to make it work. But when there's nothing worth salvaging, no definitive moments to look back on and say, 'this is why I married him, this is why I love him,' it's impossible to keep a marriage alive.''

He leaned toward her, just a fraction, but enough to make her body warm with want. As much as common sense told her to move away, to keep her chest from brushing against his, she didn't want to. She'd never admitted her frustrations about Todd to anyone—even Carmella—and she needed to know she could trust him.

Even though he hadn't been able to trust her.

His next question made her wonder if he could read minds. "Emily, I hate to ask, but what does your marriage to Todd have to do with the personnel files?''

"You know Carmella and I went into six files."

"Right."

"Think back about six months. What did all of you have in common?''

"Already asked myself that question. Came up blank.'' He studied her face, as if he'd find the clues in her look. "We're all senior management, except for Reed Connors, who probably will be soon enough. And six months ago, we were all single. But—''

"But. That's just it. The big but.''

"The big—?'' His jaw dropped as understanding dawned. They'd all married or gotten engaged in the last six months. Everyone but him.

"My father desperately wants me to marry someone at Wintersoft. Someone who'd love the company as much as they love me, and who'd be willing to take over its management someday. He was planning to drop hints to you—and the others—about asking me out on a date. And I just couldn't let that happen. It'd be mortifying. For everyone.''

"So you and Carmella—?''

"In most cases. Well, not really with Grant and Ariana. And only a little with Reed.'' She felt her face heat as she continued, "I know, it was rotten of me. I hate, hate, hate to get involved in people's personal lives. Matchmaking isn't my style. But after what happened with Todd—''

"You didn't want your father to go matchmaking

for you, so you beat him to the punch. Read up on everyone, and tried to find someone appropriate to keep them occupied so your father would leave them alone.''

She grimaced. "More or less. I'm sorry, Jack. I know it was wrong. But I didn't know what else to do. Last September, Carmella overheard him telling my aunt he planned to get me married as soon as possible. I tried talking to my father about it, pointing out that, *hello,* I'm a grown woman and can make my own decisions, but he wouldn't listen.''

A booming laugh burst from Jack, startling her. "Whoa. Now I'm beginning to understand. Is that why you brought Steven Hansen to the company's charity ball last September?''

"So you *did* know! I thought you were looking at me funny that night.''

"That Steven's gay? Of course. One, he's not good at hiding it. And two, I'd met him once before, at a conference in New York. I saw him out with a date afterward. I believe the man's name was Irving.''

Emily dropped her head back against his arm and moaned. "Okay, *now* I'm embarrassed.''

"Don't be. And please say that's why you brought Marco Valenti to your dad's last dinner party.''

"He's not gay.''

"No, but he's scum. Where women are concerned at least. I just couldn't imagine you dating him.''

"I know," she let out a deep breath. "But I had to bring someone, and I knew Steven would show his, ah, true colors at some point if he was forced to sit through a long dinner party. But if I didn't bring a date, my dad would've been cornering every single male at Wintersoft. I'd have died if he'd approached you. And Marco was the only guy I knew I could ask at the last minute who'd accept."

He squeezed her hand. "Parents do embarrassing things. I think that's part of the parent job description. But I appreciate that, in a very warped way, you were trying to defend us all from your father. I'm not sure any of us could have said no."

She tried to ignore the warmth of his hand on hers. Leaning closer, his mouth only inches from hers, he asked, "So, who were you and Carmella planning to hook me up with in your little matchmaking plan?"

"Heidi Davis?" she joked as nerves got the better of her. The intern, just out of high school, was nearly half Jack's age, and usually carried a copy of the latest teen magazine in her bag, mooning over young actors at every opportunity.

"Well, we know how badly she wants to be married. But don't you think I'm a little, um, *tall* for her?"

"Yeah, tall. Way too tall."

"Really," his eyes locked with hers, and he licked his lips. "Who did you have in mind?"

"No one," she managed to whisper. "We'd given up on you."

"Didn't find anything in my file?"

"Nope. And we couldn't imagine a woman who'd

be a good fit for you. You're a pretty private person, Jack Devon.'' His face was so close to hers, it was all she could do not to jerk away. Or lean in and kiss him.

''What if I said that you might be a good fit?''

''I'd say, 'I swore I'd never date anyone from the company again.' Then I'd say, 'I don't know a thing about you.'''

''Wrong. You know I can out-ski you,'' his lips moved across her cheek, not kissing, just touching. Teasing. ''You know I respect your business judgment. You know I can cook.''

''Sort of.'' Her breath hitched in her throat as his mouth moved to the edge of hers. ''I've only seen you make garlic bread.''

''And you know that kiss in the kitchen the other night wasn't just to prove a business point. And you know you kissed me back and enjoyed it way more than you're willing to let on. And you're willing to do it again.''

Her eyes fluttered shut as his lips finally met hers, sending warm rivers of heat through her entire body, melting away the aches and pains of an afternoon of hard skiing. Washing away the urge to tell him this wasn't right, no matter how strong the attraction between them.

But whoa, did he know how to kiss. His mouth set hers on fire, and without allowing herself to think about it, she met his tongue with hers and splayed her hands across his chest, then over his strong, protective shoulders, pulling him closer, urging him to continue despite all reason.

She didn't resist as he eased her down on the sofa, careful not to bump her ankle. His body pressed against hers, the fit unbelievable. She breathed in the scent of him, and as one of his hands moved down the side of her body, massaging her ribs, her waist, then her hip, she allowed her hands to drift down his back to his firm rear.

He moaned into her mouth, the low sound nearly sending her over the edge.

Making love to this man would be a dream.

Emily shifted underneath Jack, giving herself enough wiggle room to pull at his navy sweater and the tail of the T-shirt he wore underneath. Rewarded by the feel of his warm, smooth skin beneath her fingertips, she leaned her head back, allowing him to kiss her throat while she dug her fingers into the muscles of his back.

"Jack—" His name popped from her mouth in an involuntary groan.

His mouth froze against her neck, his body stilled. "Second thoughts?" he asked, his voice hesitant, just above a whisper.

She reached up, forked her fingers through his mussed, dark hair. "This is really stupid, you know."

For all his passion, for all his obvious desire to kiss her, to make love to her now, she knew something held him back. Otherwise, he'd have kissed her full-tilt during their encounter in the kitchen. Some reason he was either forgetting—or ignoring—right now, in the heat of the moment.

She had to be the reasonable one, to give him the chance to reconsider before they got in over their heads. Or did something they might both regret.

"Should I stop?" He raised his head just enough so she could see a flash of doubt in his dark eyes. "Your father doesn't have spy equipment in here, I hope."

"No, he doesn't." Oh, to hell with reason. "And don't you dare stop."

Chapter Seven

Jack's eyes darkened. He opened his mouth, as if about to ask Emily if she was certain, but when she silenced him with a nod, he closed his eyes and kissed her again.

Every fiber of her body heated as Jack's mouth connected with hers and his late-day stubble rubbed against her cheeks and chin. As wrong as this was, her body never felt so right.

She sank into the soft leather of the sofa as Jack swept the throw pillows out from behind her, giving him the ability to fork his fingers into her hair, to tug just enough to loosen her braid and send the elastic somewhere into the cushions.

His body gave a sudden, involuntary shake as she moved her lips just enough to brush the skin on his cheek.

"I'm going to have a hard time keeping my hands

off you in the booth tomorrow,'' he whispered. ''This feels way too good.''

Against her better judgment, she answered, ''We'll have to make up for it at the end of the day, then.''

He grunted his agreement as he kissed her shoulder, then eased his body down hers and slid her shirt just high enough to reveal the bottom of her black bra.

''I almost did this when we were in the kitchen,'' he admitted, pushing the lace aside. ''But I knew if I started unbuttoning your blouse, I wouldn't have wanted to stop.''

Emily sucked in a deep breath as his warm mouth found her nipple. ''Good thing,'' she managed, barely able to breathe as wave after wave of sensation rushed through her, ''because I wouldn't have wanted you to.''

She squeezed her eyes shut and arched against him. In all her time with Todd, she'd never wanted him even half as much as she wanted Jack at this moment. She buried her fingers in Jack's dark hair and hitched her good leg around his hip, savoring the feel of his tongue against her breast.

Oh, yes. She could make love to this man. No matter what the risks to her heart, or to her career. For just one night of pure bliss…

The phone rang, snapping her mind back to reality.

''Ignore it,'' he whispered, bringing his lips back to hers. She tuned out the phone and returned Jack's kiss, but a few rings later, her father's voice echoed through the room, killing her mood as he left a message on the machine.

"Hope you two are having fun and staying out of trouble," his familiar voice boomed, sending both Jack and Emily into a fit of laughter. "I'll be in the office for another half hour, then I'll have my cell. Please call the minute you get this—I have some new information about the investment bankers I think you'll want for tomorrow."

She sighed. Jack dropped his head to rest his forehead against hers. His eyes were half-open, dazed, and he gave her a lingering kiss, sucking in her bottom lip as a sweet torment, then letting her go.

A slow, seductive smile spread across his face. "Think he'd have called if he really knew what we were up to?"

"No way. He'd be on the phone with the nearest judge trying to get him over here to marry us. This is Nevada, you know—the official state of quickie marriages. And my dad's a desperate man."

Jack laughed as he eased away from her. "Guess we should call him back. If we don't, he'll start to wonder. He has our schedule, so he knows the trade show ended hours ago."

Emily agreed, knowing just what her father would wonder. "Why don't you call? I'll get the pizza and load up the movie." Not that she wanted to eat pizza or watch a movie anymore. She'd rather return to what they were doing before the phone rang.

His hand went to her calf, his fingers tracing lazy circles. "Your ankle's all right?"

"Fine."

He gave her one final, devastating look before crossing the room and picking up the phone to dial. Emily smiled to herself as she tossed the pillows back onto the sofa. Maybe they'd get the chance to knock them off again later. At least she hoped so.

Jack erased the message on the machine as he waited for the Wintersoft switchboard operator to page Lloyd, who apparently wasn't at his desk. Emily glanced up, and saw that he'd been watching her as she tidied up. Despite knowing it would probably bolster his ego to no end, she was unable to keep a self-satisfied smile from her face, or to stop her eyes from roaming over his long, muscled body. He winked, and the simple act made her cheeks heat.

Maybe she'd made a mistake in trying so hard not to like Jack, allowing her past to color what could be a thrilling future. Todd Baxter might have married her out of sheer ambition, then attempted to ruin her career when their marriage went bust, but Jack and Todd were entirely different men.

Perhaps—just perhaps—she should take a chance and explore their obvious attraction. Unlike Todd, Jack respected her. He'd treat her as an equal, he'd never gossip about their relationship, and she'd know in her gut he wasn't dating her just because she was Lloyd Winters's daughter.

And there was that heartstopping zing she felt every time she so much as looked at him. How could she ever share this kind of sexual chemistry with another man?

She'd need to be careful not to let on to her father until she was certain a relationship between her and Jack would last, though. And she'd try once again to convince her dad that she didn't *need* a husband to feel complete, that there was a huge difference between needing a man to make you feel secure and wanting one to share your life as a partner.

Jack finally got her father on the line and looked away from the living room to scribble a few lines on the notepad beside the phone. He returned to the sofa just as Emily got the video fast-forwarded past the previews. He gave her a slow, wicked grin just before putting his arm around her and settling in to watch the movie, a paper plate with pizza balanced on his lap.

"What?" she couldn't help but ask.

"It's a good thing you and Carmella quit while you were ahead, or we never would have had this evening. I'd have been hiding out, trying to avoid phone calls from Heidi Davis wanting to know if I'd go with her to the prom."

The opening credits began to roll, and he laughed aloud. "I could picture it now, you encouraging me to take Heidi's calls, while I scrounged around trying to look too busy to answer the phone."

"I don't think I could stand to torture you that way." Emily pulled a slice of pizza from the box onto her own plate, then scooted closer to him on the couch, so his thigh brushed up against hers. "Besides, Heidi is one of those women whose entire world view is colored by her desire to be married, at least at this point in her life. With a little more experience, she'll realize how strong she is on her own. If you think about the other couples Carmella and I set up, you'll notice there wasn't a desperate woman in the bunch.''

He took a bite of pizza, then shook his head. ''You wouldn't have had to worry about me with Heidi. No matter what you and Carmella had done to set me up—with anyone—it never would have worked. I learned long, long ago that I'm not marriage material.''

Emily's heart dropped to the pit of her stomach even as Jack's arm tightened around her. ''You know, it's been a long time since I've been able to just veg out and watch a movie, let alone after a great afternoon of skiing. Thanks, Emily.''

''Hey, no problem.'' Her words sounded casual, thank goodness, but her dreams of a future—any future—with Jack shattered at his statement. How could she have been so stupid?

She was no more knowledgeable about men at thirty-one—despite her experience with Todd—than nineteen-year-old Heidi. Of course Jack would think this was just a fling. She'd seen that facet of his personality in black and white, on the pages of *Boston Magazine,* but somewhere between their fantastic kisses and the exhilarating afternoon they'd had on the slopes, she'd allowed herself to forget that Jack was the let-no-one-too-close type.

She took a bite of her pizza, but hardly tasted it. She couldn't blame Jack for being casual, either. She'd as much as told him she wasn't interested in marriage when she'd revealed the purpose of the matchmaking scheme. If anything, it probably allowed him to pursue his attraction to her without fear that she'd want a long-term commitment from him.

But in her heart, she did want to be married. She wanted a house in the suburbs instead of her tiny Beacon Hill apartment. But most of all, she wanted a loving husband—someone who'd challenge her, who'd inspire her, who'd support her career—someone she could love with all her heart. In other words, the whole fairy tale. And for a moment, just for a moment, she'd allowed herself to believe she could have it all with Jack Devon.

"Hey, let's make a promise to each other," Jack said a short time later, as, on-screen, the villain crept up behind the main characters while the two were distracted by an argument. "Let's try harder these next few days not to push each other's buttons. We've been sizing each other up for months, if not years, subtly competing with each other professionally, when in reality, we were probably just dancing around the fact that we're attracted to each other and didn't know how to handle it."

"True," she admitted. "Showing off to catch each other's attention, but grating on each other at the same time. You think?"

How many times had she filed a report with her father that edged into Jack's realm of responsibility—partly to prove to her father that a daughter could be as brilliant as a son, but partly to prove her smarts to Jack? And how often had they each stayed late working at the office, not only to get ahead for themselves, but because they each knew the other was working late?

The look of understanding on his face told her all she needed to know. "So we're a team from now on?"

She turned on the sofa, so his arm was no longer looped over her shoulders. She winked, just to keep things light, then extended her hand to shake his. "Deal. A team."

Professionally. But not personally. Attraction— even an attraction like theirs, which had apparently run both ways for years—didn't guarantee a future together. Especially when one party didn't harbor dreams of having a home and family.

She jumped up to grab a second soda, telling herself it was a good thing Jack had come right out and said he wasn't marriage material. When she returned, she flopped into the chair, using her ankle as an excuse for the change of position.

She sneaked a peek at Jack a few minutes later, as the movie reached its special-effects-heavy, explosive climax, trying to assess his thoughts.

But he was sound asleep.

Emily picked up the remote and hit Rewind on the film, then hurried up to her own bed, before Jack could awaken and see her cry.

Jack glanced past the computer screen to where Emily was speaking with a representative from a large insurance company, giving the wiry, balding man the same spiel about Wintersoft's new program she'd given to four other potential clients that day.

Without thinking, Jack allowed his gaze to slide from her face down to her legs, which looked as incredible as ever, extending from her soft maroon skirt into a pair of black heels, despite the fact she'd been on her feet nearly eight hours.

How'd she do it?

The muscles down the front of Jack's legs ached so he could barely stand. Yesterday he'd been fine at the trade show, but now, forty-eight hours after their trip to the slopes, his muscles finally decided to launch their official protest.

He'd forgotten how much an afternoon of skiing took out of him, particularly when he hadn't hit the slopes in years. His usual workouts at the gym hadn't prepared him for the unpredictable motions of guiding skis through tight moguls, though the real damage had been done in his attempt to ski at his fastest without a proper warm-up, just to show off for Emily.

Then again, his hot-dogging had paid off. He and Emily had come to understand each other better, and their quickie make-out session on the couch had sent his body—and much as he hated to acknowledge it, his emotions—into overdrive. Her body melded perfectly to his, and their instant physical chemistry amazed him and left him aching for more. Never had he felt so in tune with a woman.

He'd thought he'd burst when she opted to move to the chair to support her ankle during the movie, and he'd regretted it even more last night, when they'd been so exhausted from the trade show they hadn't bothered to prepare dinner or review their files—they'd each made a beeline for their own beds.

Still, much as he'd hated it at the time, it had been a damned good thing she'd moved from the sofa to the chair after Lloyd's call, or who knows where things might've gone. He'd meant what he said about not being marriage material, but if ever a woman might make him reconsider, might make him believe he could be better at marriage than his parents had been, it would be Emily Winters.

Tonight, though, things would be different—aching muscles be damned. Tomorrow morning they'd be on a plane to Boston, and for his own sanity, he needed to explore what existed between them before they lost the chance to do so in private. He'd just be careful not to let things get too out of hand.

A safe, controlled relationship. He could have the best of both worlds with Emily—someone with a brain who set his body on fire, yet who didn't view him as some Prince Charming waiting for her at the front of a chapel, priest at the ready.

He returned his focus to the computer screen so Emily wouldn't catch him staring at her and read his thoughts. She'd come to the kitchen this morning rested and smiling, and claimed over their breakfast of toast and coffee that her ankle was back to one hundred percent. His throat had immediately tightened in response as he thought of where he'd like to see that ankle, and he'd wondered if her thoughts followed the same path as his.

Despite the potential risk to his career, he hoped so.

As he chatted with a board member from one of Wintersoft's client companies and loaded up the software for yet another demonstration, his attention kept drifting to his watch, checking to see how many more hours until he'd be back at the house—not so he could flop on the leather sofa and ease the throbbing in his quads with a handful of aspirin, but so he could be alone with Emily.

As Emily greeted another customer, a genuine smile lighting her face, he couldn't help but think of what he'd said the other night about his inability to keep his hands off her while they were at the booth.

He'd been wrong. He'd actually *under*estimated the difficulty. A difficulty she didn't seem to be having. Maybe a controlled relationship wasn't such a good idea—

"Tired today, Jack?" the client asked with a frown.

Jack cloaked his thoughts with a smile and clicked forward to the next screen. "The conference wraps up tomorrow, and today's the last day the trade show's open. Isn't everyone tired?"

The client agreed, and for the remaining hour and a half, Jack forced himself not to look in Emily's direction. When 7:00 p.m. finally rolled around, and the last of the conference attendees drifted toward the doors of the exhibition hall, he was surprised to see Emily still looking lively.

"How many cups of coffee did you have this morning?" he teased.

"Too many," she grinned and held up a steaming cup. "Mike Elliott was sweet enough to bring me another to hold me over, since he knew the show was going to run later than usual today. I'm probably going to be up all night."

"Not me," he replied, not unless he was the one keeping her up. He leaned over to disconnect the computer and grab the paperwork required to ship the equipment back to Boston. Thank goodness Carmella had organized everything in advance so all they had to do was sign the forms for the delivery service. "I'm looking forward to spending a nice, long evening on the sofa. Or maybe out in that hot tub I saw on your father's deck." He gave her a look meant to tell her that a dip would wake him up just enough to continue what they'd started two nights ago.

"I think I have a better idea."

He tried to quell his instant arousal. "You thinking of something specific?"

"Yep. But first things first. Let's dump everything at the house and call my father to let him know how the last day went. He's on Boston time, remember, so I want to get that taken care of before he goes to bed or we pursue our own plans."

Jack agreed, his mind already racing ahead to guess just what those plans might be.

Man, could her father talk. And talk some more. As Emily punched the telephone buttons, finally ending the teleconference she and Jack had with Lloyd, she forced herself not to groan at the hour. She'd really wanted more time tonight.

"Well, what's your plan now?" Jack's rich, enticing voice made it clear his thoughts had traveled the same path as hers. Well, not precisely the *same* path. As he hooked one hand around her waist from behind, she said an inward prayer of thanks she'd come up with an idea for a fun evening—one that would convince him she was the fun-loving, relaxed woman he'd kissed the other night, yet keep him from kissing her again.

If he did, she knew her heart would be lost. And she didn't want to lose her heart ever again without knowing the man involved felt the same way about her.

"Let me run up to my room for a sec, then I'll tell you," she teased, then raced to her room. Ten minutes later, she returned in black slacks and a flirty, but not too revealing, dusty blue top that puckered at the bodice.

He raised an eyebrow, making his approval obvious, but said nothing.

"I think we're due for a night on the town," Emily announced. "So here's my plan. We start out at the El Dorado. Maybe catch dinner at the Roxy Bistro." Intimate, but not so romantic that if they ran into any conference attendees, they'd look as if they were out on a date. "Then we go next door to the Silver Legacy, where I can introduce you to my favorite slots. My dad and I have been here so many times I can tell you exactly which machines are hot. Then we finish up back at the El Dorado. They have the best craps dealers. Even if we don't play, it's a blast just to stand tableside and cheer for everyone.''

A shadow crept into Jack's gray eyes, and Emily immediately knew she'd said something wrong. ''Unless that's a problem? Are you too tired to go out?''

''No. Not too tired, it's just...'' He shrugged and looked toward the windows, despite the fact the late hour made it impossible to see anything besides the occasional light across the lake.

''Let's brainstorm and come up with something else to do. Maybe we can rent another movie? Or take a drive around the lake?'' He ran a hand over his jaw, then turned back toward her, the shadow in his eyes replaced with unmistakable desire. ''I wouldn't mind having a quiet night to ourselves.''

Panic swept through Emily. How could one man be so-o-o tempting? Or so, so dangerous to her heart?

''How about a compromise?'' she tried. ''We take the long way around before going into Reno—maybe see a little of the lake at night? We can see a movie anytime.''

Her breath hitched as she spoke, despite her attempt to remain calm. She couldn't possibly stay in the house with him. The last two days had just about killed her—watching him work his magic in the booth with their clients and partners, observing him in silence last night from a darkened corner of the living room as he'd tiptoed into the kitchen wearing only his pajama pants to grab a late-night snack, long after he thought she'd gone to bed.

She studied his face, her heart aching with longing and a healthy dose of fear. His expression made it clear he had no desire to leave the house, but they both knew what would happen if they got within arm's reach of each other, and once it did...well, she doubted they'd stop. There wouldn't be a phone call from her father to jerk her back to reality, and frankly, she knew they'd both ignore any interruptions. Just one kiss, one touch...if she had the chance to run her hands over his strong shoulders again or, as she'd dreamed about last night after seeing him in the kitchen, to skim them over the beautifully sculpted planes of his rock-hard abs, she'd be lost.

And what then? He read her so well, he'd know she wanted a commitment from him. He'd see the dreams of family life, of weekend barbecues and kids' soccer games. He'd bolt, their work relationship would end up more strained than ever, and she'd be heartbroken.

Worst of all, everyone in the office would eventually find out, and all hell would break loose. She could almost hear the gossip in the ladies' room and in the elevators, everyone whispering in excited tones about how the boss's daughter had gotten involved with Jack Devon, and it turned out badly. Again. All the respect she'd worked so hard to build since her breakup with Todd—all her long hours of work, all her accomplishments—would be forgotten in an instant. Not only by her colleagues, but by her father, driving home his belief that he needed a son, not a daughter, to run the company once he decided to retire.

Jack would come out of it looking like a total stud or a cad. She wasn't sure which, and she didn't want to know.

He took a few steps toward her, making the open living room feel more closed-in than ever. Little crinkles appeared at the corners of his eyes, and Emily fought to keep still as he reached out and touched her hair, smoothing a few strands back behind her ear. "I'd prefer not to gamble."

What else was there to do in Reno at night? Well, besides what Jack obviously had in mind. Gathering every ounce of fortitude, she turned away from him and grabbed her purse from the coffee table. "C'mon. It'll be a blast, I'm telling you." She hoped her words sounded airy. "The food at the Roxy's to die for. And I'll even spot you ten bucks on the slots. What have you got to lose?"

She was halfway up the staircase when she realized Jack hadn't moved.

She spun around, figuring she'd tease him into following along, just as he had on the ski slopes, but the hard look in his eyes stopped her cold, despite his light tone. "No thanks. I have no desire, none whatsoever, to spend even one minute in some smoke-filled casino full of people wasting away every last dime they have."

Was he kidding? Confusion kept her from replying immediately, and he blew by her up the stairs, pausing at the door to his room. "When you decide what you'd like to do tonight, you know where to find me.''

He left his door ajar in a clear invitation, but Emily couldn't believe what she'd just witnessed, or the disapproving tone in his voice. What was with him? Did he really feel so strongly about staying in tonight that he was willing to make her feel like a heel for wanting to go gambling, just to convince her not to leave?

Or was this some kind of test? Pushing her to the limit to see how much control he had over their situation?

She stared at his bedroom door for a moment. It would be so, so easy to walk in there. To spend a night in absolute heaven, and not regret it until she returned to Boston.

Closing her eyes, she took a deep breath, and unbidden, the image of Todd leaning against her office door popped into her head. His belittling tone, telling her she was frigid, and insinuating that she wasn't good for anything except getting him ahead at the company. That she didn't deserve the respect of her colleagues. That she was nothing more than daddy's little girl. That she'd be successful and happy if she'd only do what he told her.

As she opened her eyes and looked at Jack's door, a lone tear burned down her cheek, and she immediately swiped it away.

No way on earth was she going to let a man, *any* man—her father, Todd or even Jack—dictate what she could and couldn't do. She was sick and tired of the men in her life *controlling* her life.

She climbed the last few stairs to the upper landing and took a final, long look at Jack's door, allowing her determination to build. Grabbing the keys to the truck from the hook beside the front door, she said just loud enough for Jack to hear, "I'll leave the sedan in the garage for you if you want to take that drive around the lake. I'll be in Reno."

Then without looking back, she strode out the door.

Chapter Eight

Emily flagged down one of the El Dorado's waitresses and ordered a vodka tonic, then repositioned her stool in front of a blinking Fireball slot machine. She fed three coins into the slot, trying to ignore the lean brunette's too-tight top and barely there hot pants as she scribbled down the drink order, along with one for the elderly woman occupying the stool to Emily's right. Maybe the bite of alcohol, even the watered-down variety the casinos served to anyone actively gambling, might take away the sting of Jack's rejection.

How could he be such a jerk?

Then again, how could she blame him, when she'd brought it upon herself?

She punched the button to set the reels rolling, then watched as the images spun, slowed, then clunked to a stop. Nothing.

She sighed, then plunked another three quarters from her plastic cup into the machine, this time winning four back.

As she continued to play, keeping the cup bearing the casino's logo in her lap so she could monitor her spending and be certain not to go over her forty-dollar limit, images of Jack flashed through her mind—his hand snaking around her waist, the invitation in his gaze, and then the icy edge he'd developed when she'd suggested hitting the town.

The waitress returned, and Emily took a long, cool sip of her vodka tonic, letting the liquid run down her throat to soothe her frustration. Didn't work. She pushed the play button again, sending lightning strikes and flaming balls of fire whizzing in front of her.

As cutting as Jack's look had been, it couldn't have come from the simple fact she wanted to gamble. Jack was a risk-taker himself, always going for broke to land a new client. Or this week, tackling the toughest ski slopes just to keep up with her, even though she knew he didn't ski regularly. That was a lot more dangerous than walking into a casino with forty bucks in quarters knowing you'd lose them. What was the difference between visiting a casino and going to a movie and buying popcorn and drinks for two? It was entertainment spending, pure and simple.

"Men," she muttered to herself as she continued to watch the dizzying rows of bombs, rockets and fireballs in front of her. Clearly Jack was used to women whose primary goal was to keep him at home, where they could indulge in all he had to offer.

She grunted, then took another sip of her drink.

Jack just couldn't take no for an answer, that was all. And it wasn't as if she'd even said no! She just needed some space—some time out where she could enjoy his company but keep her hands to herself until she could decide how to handle all this. She had to keep herself from making another Todd Baxter-caliber mistake.

After another losing spin, she cashed out on the machine and wandered aimlessly around the casino, grabbing a second drink—this time a simple ice water—from a passing waitress.

She finally stopped at the end of one of the casino's craps tables, and within minutes, managed to get involved in the lively game. Despite deciding not to play—she only had a rudimentary understanding of how the game worked—she enjoyed watching the crowd root for a certain number to appear on a roll of the dice. Before long, she'd finished her water, grabbed another, and joined in the crowd, cheering for the good rolls, and booing and hissing the bad ones. Bells rang somewhere nearby, then she heard a chorus of cheers go up behind her as group of twentysomethings gathered around a winning slot machine.

A man standing next to her at the table asked her to blow on his dice for luck, and she obliged. Why not? This was what she needed—a respite from the stress of work, a little time to relax and do nothing in particular. A band was about to play in the far corner of the casino, adding to the festive ambience. If Jack didn't want to be part of it, so be it.

"Are you feeling quite lucky?"

The accented voice behind her was so quiet she almost didn't turn around. When she did, she couldn't keep the surprise from her face. "Randall! You haven't flown back to New York yet?"

He shook his head. "First thing in the morning. So," he gestured toward the table. "Are you winning?"

She held up her cup full of quarters. "Not playing. I'm a slot machine kind of girl."

"I don't blame you." He glanced over her head at the green felt-topped craps table, where the dealer was taking bets and placing chips on the appropriate spots. "I never understood this game."

"And here I thought you were a numbers man," she teased.

His laugh was deep and sexy as he replied, "Nope. I'm a leg man."

Okay, Jack was right. Randall was definitely flirting. "Well, you should be having a field day here. I've never seen shorts as short as the waitresses are wearing."

As if on cue, a petite blond waitress appeared at Randall's elbow. He ordered a martini for himself, and since Emily's water glass was empty, she asked for another.

"No, I don't imagine waitresses anywhere dress quite like they do in the Reno casinos," he commented once the tiny blonde was out of earshot. "Except perhaps Las Vegas. Another American city I've yet to visit." He cleared his throat as he continued in his thick British accent, "But I'm looking forward to seeing you in Boston. I do believe the board will follow my recommendation."

"Time will tell," she smiled, shifting back to her professional mindset. "I truly believe it'll save ABG money, and you'll see the returns immediately."

Randall put a hand on her shoulder and spun her back toward the craps table so she could watch the players once more. "You don't need to sell me on it, Emily. You're truly a company girl, aren't you?"

A light laugh bubbled from her as he leaned over her shoulder to watch another player throw the dice. "Hard not to be when your father owns the company."

"Enjoy your night off," he advised. "I plan to."

"All right, then." She handed the dealer two rolls of quarters from her cup, cashing them in for chips. "I will."

Jack flinched at the sound of the front door slamming shut behind Emily.

What is my freakin' problem?

He cursed aloud, drowning out the familiar roar as Emily started up her father's truck. He flopped onto his back on the king-size bed, punching the mattress with his fist.

Emily. Emily was his problem. His attraction for her ran bone-deep, despite knowing he'd make a lousy husband, and in a fit of anger, he'd been insane enough to let her go.

Why couldn't she just stay the hell out of the casinos? He'd go anywhere—a restaurant, a bowling alley, even some dive bar—anywhere but a casino.

He let out a half groan, half growl, and pushed himself to his feet. Striding into the bathroom, he grabbed his toothbrush and scrubbed his teeth harder than necessary. She wanted to leave? Fine. He'd hit the hay and forget about her. Forget what she did to him, forget that for the first time in his life, he was tempted to pursue a serious relationship with a woman.

Two hours later, he groaned again and rolled over.

Emily wasn't his problem. His past—and his own hang-ups about his parents' marriage and his father's addiction—were.

He glanced at the clock. Nearly midnight, meaning it was way, way too late to phone his mother in Florida. He wanted to hear her voice, if only to know that she was as happy and well-adjusted as she claimed to be, and that his father hadn't screwed up her life for the long term. Or, if he was honest, to draw on her deep reserve of inner strength and use it to get through the rest of the night.

He sat up in the bed, and while he fished his jeans from the footboard, he repeated his mother's words over and over.

Jack Devon, you are not *your father.*

He wanted to believe it, desperately. But he knew in his gut that he harbored the same compulsive drive and single-minded determination to succeed that his father had once possessed. He'd never have advanced as far and as fast at Wintersoft if he didn't have that competitive spirit touching everything he did, pushing him to do just one step better than the next guy, and to outperform himself every year.

If his father could fall so far, allowing his focus to shift when he was just weeks from grasping the brass ring upon which he'd fixed his gaze for years and years, then what was to stop him from doing the same?

Or from treating the woman in his life—whether it was Emily, as he wished it could be, or anyone else— as though she was no better than a clod of dirt on his shoe? Certainly his father hadn't treated his mother with half the respect she deserved.

Dammit, he needed control, at least in one area of his life, even if his father couldn't achieve it.

Yanking a black turtleneck sweater over his head as he went, Jack strode out of his room, pulled on his coat, then scoured the foyer until he located the keys to Lloyd's sedan, hanging on a hook near the front door. He might have his father's destructive impulses, but he'd be damned if he'd treat Emily with even a shred of the callousness his father exhibited toward his mom.

Even if it did mean facing a boisterous casino and all its temptations.

Almost an hour later, as he strode through the Silver Legacy's lower level and scanned the rows of gamblers plunking their money into machines, he knew he'd done the right thing. He could handle this. He wouldn't stop and look at the machines, was all. Wouldn't listen to the casino employees positioned near the doors and escalators, offering coupons for one free pull at the slots, or two free chips to play roulette.

A quarter rolled in front of him on the burgundy carpet, circling to a stop near his shoe. He knelt and retrieved it for a woman perched on a red vinyl stool at the end of a row of slots, playing a machine touting itself as a provider of Riches! Riches! Riches!

"Thank you, sweetie," she said, giving him a warm smile and tucking her silver hair into place as he handed her the quarter. "I have so much trouble bending to the floor. Bet this one's lucky now."

"Hope so." A perfectly normal woman. Not a drunk. Not a hoodlum.

Not all gamblers are morally bankrupt, Devon.

He strode along a few more rows, concluding that Emily wasn't in the casino, then took the escalator, climbing the steps by twos as he went, to the second floor, where a bridge connected the Silver Legacy to the El Dorado. In the lobby, he passed an oversize water fountain, complete with a giant sculpture of Poseidon guiding his horses into a battle at sea. He scanned the signs on the beige marble walls and noticed a restaurant tucked into the corner of the lobby. He approached the woman at the hostess's stand, but within a minute, he ascertained that Emily hadn't stopped to dine at the Roxy Bistro, either.

Turning his back on the softly lit restaurant, he

cursed under his breath. How could he have passed up a night with Emily in that place? Even if it wasn't as intimate as spending an evening wrapped in each other's arms on the sofa at Lloyd's place, it had romance and serenity written all over it.

His stomach tightened again with desire as he jogged down the stairs leading from the lobby into the El Dorado's casino. Could Emily possibly want him as badly as he did her?

Could he risk a relationship with her?

He studied the rows of gamblers, all lined up at slot machines laid out in a similar pattern to those in the Silver Legacy. People cradled cups of coins in the crooks of their arms as they wandered the floor, searching for a machine that might be lucky, or juggled handfuls of chips as they gathered in boisterous groups around the blackjack tables and the roulette wheel. An aura of excitement and fun permeated the room, and he took a deep breath to calm his agitated nerves.

He'd only spent a few hours in a casino, once, as a teenager. The smell of cigarette smoke and desperation had overwhelmed him then, like a palpable weight settling onto his shoulders, threatening to knock him to the red-carpeted floor and stomp him into nothingness.

But now, as an adult, he finally understood the attraction, as well as his own ability to resist it. If you approached gambling with the right mindset, as most of these people apparently did, then it was nothing more than a form of entertainment, as simple as attending a movie or going to see a Bruins game at the Fleet Center.

No, he wasn't his father. He'd never lose his life here, just as Emily would never lose her life here.

He walked along the rows of machines, his steps lighter as he scanned the crowd, hoping to catch a glimpse of Emily's soft brown hair or the incredibly sexy blue top she'd been wearing. He stopped short at the sound of her laughter, spun around, and headed in the direction of the craps tables, dodging casino patrons as he wove his way through the crowded aisles.

Please, he prayed, let her forgive me. Then, perhaps, they could set things right between them for once and for all.

When he saw her, his heart soared—until he saw a blond head just behind hers. She was leaning over the craps table, nursing a tall glass with ice and lime he guessed didn't contain water. Randall Wellingby's hand rested on her shoulder.

And she'd just lost a huge pile of chips.

"Emily."

Emily jerked at the sound of Jack's voice behind her. He sported a pair of loafers, jeans and a casual black turtleneck sweater. Yet his coat rested haphazardly on his shoulders, and his hair looked as if he'd been dragged out of bed against his will.

"Jack?" She couldn't help but allow her surprise into her tone. "I thought you were—" She remembered Randall's presence at the last minute and finished, "uh, working. What's up?"

"Nothing important," he replied, though his harried look made the lie obvious. "Just thought I'd get away from the grind for a while." Jack glanced at Randall. "Having fun, I hope?"

There wasn't a hint of jealousy in Jack's eyes or in his voice, but Emily could feel it rolling off him in waves. Or perhaps it was disapproval. After this evening's blowup, she wasn't sure how to interpret Jack anymore. Not that she'd ever had a handle on him in the first place.

"Sure am," Randall laughed, oblivious to the tension between Jack and Emily. "Emily here turned twenty bucks into nearly four hundred."

"And just lost a hundred," she rolled her eyes.

"The other three hundred is safely stashed," Randall noted, eyeing her cup, which now held a sizable number of chips, in addition to her rolls of quarters. He turned to her, then dropped an unexpected kiss on her cheek. "I have to go. My flight's quite early. But I'll call you when I know my plans for Boston, or when I hear from the board."

"Thanks, Randall," she nodded, all too aware of being under Jack's observation and knowing what he must think, especially after he'd pointed out—correctly—that Randall had the hots for her. "I look forward to talking to you again."

As soon as Randall disappeared into the crowd, Jack grabbed her hand. "Let's get out of here."

"On one condition."

He raised an eyebrow, but didn't let go of her hand. "Yeah?"

"I think you owe me an apology."

He stunned her by agreeing. "You're right. But not here."

She nodded, and followed him out without bothering to cash in her chips. She'd do it tomorrow, before they left for the airport, or give them to her father to cash in, since he planned to come to Reno himself in only a few weeks. When they got to the parking lot, however, she realized the apology would have to wait—Jack had driven her father's sedan, which was parked two spaces away from the truck.

"Meet you at my dad's?"

"You're—you're sober enough to drive?" She could see in his eyes that he hated to ask.

"One very weak vodka tonic, right when I got here. And nothing but water since."

He nodded, and she couldn't help but notice his relief. "I'll be right behind you." He opened the door to the truck and, without another word, handed her in. By the time they arrived at the house, nearly an hour later, she could hardly keep still.

The moment the door closed behind them and she'd shrugged out of her coat, she turned to face him. "Care to explain what happened here tonight?" At the somber look on his face, she added, "I promise to hear you out, whatever it is you need to say."

He took off his coat and looped it carelessly over a chair near the front door, then took her hand once again, leading her downstairs to the couch. Without thinking, she bit her lip. What could Jack have to say that was so serious?

And would this be the last time he'd ever hold her hand? She glanced at their intertwined fingers as they sat facing each other on the sofa.

"I shouldn't have been so harsh about staying here and renting a movie," he started, his gaze following hers to their hands. "I know we promised not to push each other's buttons the other night, but, well, gambling is one of mine. Probably my worst. You couldn't have known that, though. I should have said something instead of getting hacked off."

His hand tightened around hers, and she saw the apology in his eyes before he leaned in close enough to kiss her—a safe, gentle peck on the cheek. "It won't happen again, Emily."

His warm breath washed against her face. It would be so easy to turn her face to his, to meet his lips with hers, but she couldn't. Not yet.

"Why gambling, Jack?"

He let out a puff of air and gave her a reluctant grin as he sat back. "Why did I know you were going to ask that?"

"I don't want to push buttons. But, well, I have no idea what's going on with us. What to call this." She put her free hand over their interlaced fingers and met his gaze. "But I feel like I should know. You know?" She knew she sounded like an idiot, her words tripping over each other as she strove for clarification.

Jack didn't seem bothered, though. He eased his hand from hers and leaned back against the arm of the couch, sitting sideways so he faced her. "My father was a gambling addict. My mother called it electronic morphine—the drive to put just one more dollar in a slot machine, or to park himself at the sportsbook places and gamble just one more mortgage payment in hopes his horse or his football team would make it all better."

"Like a junkie needing his fix," Emily sighed, instantly realizing why he'd been so upset, and how deep Jack's pain had to run, though at the same time relieved he didn't have a gambling problem himself. "People make light of gambling, I know, but from the time we started coming here, my dad made it abundantly clear that anyone going into the casino had to set limits before walking in the door. He made no bones about the fact that gambling can cause a lot of problems." She hoped she sounded sympathetic, but not pitying, as she added, "It can even ruin families."

"Damn straight."

"So," she frowned, "why couldn't you just tell me that? I mean, I understand wanting to encourage me to stay here to avoid the whole topic, but when I balked, why not just explain? It's not something you should be embarrassed about. And I won't think less of you."

"It's not you. I've never told a soul." He forked his fingers through his short, dark hair, then met her gaze. "My dad and I were a lot alike. He was a determined, ambitious man. Never had a thing given to him. He never finished high school—dropped out when he and my mom had to get married." He shot her a wicked grin and jerked a thumb toward his chest. "That's what you did in South Boston in those days. But he landed a job at the Quincy Shipyards and worked his tail off, first at minimum wage, then slowly moving up to a supervisory position. At night, he got his GED, and was even putting aside money to attend community college. Just to make things better for my mom and me."

"Sounds like a hard worker. And like he loved you very much."

"He did. Until one afternoon, he was checking the mail and found a coupon for a free dinner at a brand-new casino down in Connecticut. A bunch of his co-workers received them, too. Since one of the guys was getting married, they all decided to take the coupons down to the new casino and have the bachelor party there, since dinner would be free."

Emily's heart wrenched for Jack. "And that was the beginning?"

Jack nodded. "My father loved the place. Absolutely loved it. Like a kid going to Disney World with unlimited tickets for ice cream and snacks, not to mention all the rides. But unlike a kid with ice cream, he never got that sensation of 'too much of a good thing,' you know? Within a few months, he discovered sports betting. And the dog tracks. The money he'd set aside for community college was gone, and he had this insane idea that he could win it all back. So he kept betting. Casino gambling was illegal in Massachusetts, so when he couldn't travel to casinos on the weekends, he started playing poker. He had a knack for it, and it gave him that same thrill. And to make things worse, he started winning back some of what he'd lost, so he convinced himself he could bet bigger and win bigger. And you know what they say about how the mighty fall.''

"What did your mother do?"

"At first, nothing. She thought it was a phase, something to help him get through his job stress. He was so close to being promoted, to being able to manage his section at the shipyards, and he'd been dying to get that position for years. But soon he was cutting work to gamble. And after he started playing poker with the sharks, he really went downhill—started missing mortgage payments, too. That's when she tried to intervene, and it got ugly. They kept breaking up and getting back together. They even tried going through gambling addiction programs together.''

Emily scooted closer to Jack. "Nothing worked?"

He fiddled with the neck of his sweater, then dropped his hands to his lap, and she knew he was fighting to keep the regret and sadness from his expression. "No. Not until he died. I loved my father, don't get me wrong. But when he passed away, it was the best thing for my mother. It freed her.''

"Jack, that's so sad. I take it she's all right now?"

"She's living in a condo in Florida. And last year she got married again, to a man I really admire and who appreciates her. So yes, she's all right.''

"That's good to hear." She hesitated a second,

then said, "I'm sorry I pushed the point about going to the casino tonight. If I'd known—"

"I didn't want you to know. Think about it, Emily. I'm very much like my father—determined, stubborn. Too much so. The last thing I want anyone, especially anyone at work, to know is that my father couldn't handle money. Do you think I'd be trusted with handling deals worth millions of dollars?"

Before she could argue, he leaned forward, his lean, hard body filling the small space between them on the sofa. "I don't want to test the theory by letting people know, all right? Going to the casino tonight turned out to be a good thing for me. I realized, for the first time ever, that I can walk through one without having some overriding urge to play a machine or plunk my 401(k) funds down on a table. I know it sounds ridiculous to you that I worry about having that urge, but you've got to walk in my shoes to understand. Then tonight, when I saw that you were cradling a drink, and you'd just lost that huge pile of chips—"

"You instantly thought I was being careless with my money."

He nodded. "But I realized that you were watching what you lost when Randall spoke up. And I knew once I got close that you were drinking water. Not vodka or gin. No odor. Though I had to ask when we were leaving, just to be sure." He touched her hand, just enough to run his index finger along the back of her knuckles. "Before today, and before getting to know you better, I wouldn't have stopped to think. I would have made my assumptions and then embarrassed myself even worse than I did by demanding that we stay in tonight.''

"Then I'll avoid asking you to a casino in the future, if that's all right with you.''

He laughed, and the lightheartedness of it warmed her through. "Probably wise. But I'm still sorry I ruined your evening.''

"First, it wasn't ruined,'' she pointed out. "And second, even if it was, I did that myself by slamming out of here like I did. You sometimes act on gut instinct because of the way your father treated your family. Well, I sometimes do the same. I know I can't possibly compare my father to yours, but—'' A deep sigh escaped her, though she tried unsuccessfully to bite it back to keep from sounding pathetic. "Whenever a man starts trying to tell me what to do—like Todd did, or my father still sometimes does—I get agitated and do stupid things like walking out on a wonderful man.''

"I see. Your garden-variety control issues.''

She chuckled. "You've got it. Control issues. Thanks, Dr. Devon.''

The spark in his eye quieted her laughter. He reached up, gently cupping her chin, his dark gaze holding her immobile. "But what if a man asks you to kiss him? A man, I might point out, who is nothing like Todd Baxter and asks you not to think about what your father would say, or about anything that's happened with any man who's kissed you before. Do you have an issue with that?''

Chapter Nine

"In that case, he'd be asking. Not telling."

The wicked curve to Jack's mouth made her skin prickle in anticipation. He inched forward, his mouth a mere breath from hers. "So it's not a control-issue-type situation, then?"

"Mmm," she whispered as he raised his head to torment her with a soft kiss on her eyelid, then another on her cheekbone. Thoughts of her father and Todd—and her worries about Jack's ability to commit—fled as Jack's touch filled her with want. "Are you saying you need to be in control?"

"Are you?"

"This is going to be another competition, isn't it? I thought we agreed not to push each others' buttons anymore."

"Hmm," he breathed, his cheek resting against hers, his lips brushing her ear. "In that case, perhaps it's time we learned the right way to push each other's buttons.''

She was about to tease him again, but he turned, and his kiss stopped all rational thought. From the instant their lips connected, Jack made it much more than the simple kiss she'd anticipated. Every motion—from the pressure of his hands against her back to the soft sweep of his tongue against hers—made it clear that he wanted much, much more than kissing. And that he wanted it from *her*—no other woman could possibly substitute.

He moved her back against the cushions, though she gave a half-hearted push against his chest to slow him down, just to prove he hadn't completely won on the control issue. But her push turned into a caress as her fingertips lingered against his firm, muscled torso, and then wound around to his back as he eased on top of her, his hands tangled in her hair. Pinned beneath Jack, feeling the weight of him along every inch of her body as his sensuous lips explored hers, sent her hormones into overdrive.

His, too, judging from the way his body responded to their intimate contact. They'd known each other for so long—dancing around their attraction as they'd sparred over business issues in the office, resisting their impulses in the interest of keeping things professional, and keeping their dating lives sterile for their own deeply personal reasons—that to finally give in to what they'd each dreamed of made each touch, each kiss, each quiet sigh more erotic and more potent than it could possibly be with anyone else.

Emily's breath hitched in her throat as Jack's hand moved down her side, then under the fabric of her top where it had ridden up on her waist.

"I want all of you, Em," he whispered against her mouth, and when she responded by deepening their kiss, he slid her shirt a few inches higher, his hand setting her skin afire. With agonizing slowness, he lowered his head to place gentle, teasing kisses along her stomach. The thin layer of stubble dotting his cheeks and chin simultaneously tickled her and made her groan in delight. Somewhere in the back of her brain, Emily decided she would risk anything to have Jack do this to her for the rest of her life.

"You're cold." There was a smile in his whispered comment, even as he kissed her and ran his large hands over her ribcage, then under the sides of her bra. "Come on. I'll warm you up."

He cradled her, pulling her off the sofa. "I think you're doing a pretty good job already," she protested, unwilling to have his perfect body out of touch with hers.

"There's wood and newspaper next to the fireplace. It'll only take a second."

A fire? Oh, man, was he *good*. Stifling an unbidden image of the *Boston Magazine* article, and thoughts of how he'd gotten to be so good, she said, "Let me help."

Within a few minutes, flames leapt to life in the large, stone fireplace, instantly warming the room. Even as Emily replaced the fire screen, Jack pulled her away from the hearth, down onto the Mexican wool rug her mother had picked up on a vacation to Acapulco when Emily was only a toddler.

"Better?" he asked.

"Infinitely." Who wouldn't be, looking up at a face like Jack's smiling down at her, with desire filling his eyes and the red glow of a fire at his back? He kissed her again, long and slow and wet, warming her more thoroughly than the fire. No fantasy she'd ever had about Jack—and she'd had plenty over the years—lived up to the real thing. Without caring what tomorrow might bring, she reached to his waistband and tucked her fingers under the edge of his black sweater, easing it over his head.

If feeling his chest under her fingertips felt like heaven, seeing the smooth, tanned skin before her sent her right into another universe. "You're gorgeous," she couldn't help but whisper.

His grin broadened. "I'll remind you of that next time you argue with me about who should talk to a potential client." Before she could retort, he placed a finger over her lips. "Don't ever doubt yourself, Emily. You might think your father wanted a son," his voice was low and rough as he made an obvious perusal of her body, "but I can say with all authority it's a damned good thing for me he had a daughter. And not so I could try to marry into the company and run it myself, like Baxter wanted to. He wasn't nearly worthy of you."

"Thank you," Emily murmured against his finger. "Thanks for understanding."

Keeping her gaze riveted on his face, she opened

her mouth just enough to tease his finger with her tongue, then draw it into her mouth.

"It has its benefits," he managed, then bent down to kiss her again.

Emily opened her eyes the next morning, gradually registering the roughness of her mother's Mexican rug against her bare stomach and the fuzzy texture of an afghan over her shoulders and back. One of the sofa's throw pillows rested under her cheek—she wasn't sure how that got there—and Jack's arm was draped over her, his warm, solid bicep against her back, his lean fingers circling her arm.

She smiled into the pillow when she spied her top bunched up on the floor, near Jack's turtleneck sweater and his jeans. Hers remained on, but she could still feel the heat of his boxer-clad thighs against her. For two consenting adults in a romantic log home, with a burning fire behind them and a breathtaking view of Lake Tahoe spread out before them, they'd done a pretty good job of reining things in.

They'd never broached the topic of sex, though they'd gotten about as close as they could get to having it without actually *having* it. Whenever a hand had strayed into dangerous territory, or another piece of clothing had hit the floor, things shifted from fast and passionate back to slow and romantic, as if an unseen barrier stopped them from taking that final step.

Emily knew what stopped her. Todd had taken her trust and abused it. And she'd never been the one-night-stand type. If she made love to Jack Devon, it had to be body and soul, with the full knowledge she'd never again make love to another man.

And without knowing that, she'd hesitated. He'd never once told her that he'd lied, or that he'd changed his mind—about not being the marrying type.

But what had stopped him? At points where he could have coaxed her along and taken her to that final level, he'd backed off, breaking their building passion with a well-timed joke, or by simply returning to the soft, easy kisses that were his forte. Given his reputation, she'd been surprised. Her first instinct said he probably didn't have a condom with him and didn't want to risk it. But now, as she lay cuddled against his unbelievable body, listening to his slow, even breathing, she wondered if he was really the different-date-every-night sex god the magazine article portrayed him to be.

Perhaps he hadn't pushed things further because he didn't want to go there.

Easing her arm out from under his hand, she squinted at her watch. Quarter to six. Their flight was at nine, so she needed to get up and moving. No way she'd leave the house a mess, plus there was the forty-five-minute drive to the airport.

As quietly as possible, she pushed up onto her elbows, and rolled out from under Jack's arm. After making sure he was well-covered, she folded his clothes and laid them near his head, grabbed her blue top, then tiptoed up the stairs for a shower, deciding to let him sleep a while longer.

A half hour later, when she returned to make coffee, he was gone. The edges of the wool rug had been smoothed back into place, the afghan and throw pillows returned to their appropriate spots on the leather couch. Even the fireplace was clean, all the ashes swept out and placed in a separate bag inside the trash can.

Emily scanned the room again, her heart constricting when she spied a pair of frozen bagels defrosting on a plate on the granite countertop. She'd never in a million years pegged Jack as the domestic type.

"Oh, my," she exhaled as the sound of Jack's shower turning on reached her ears. What had she gotten herself into?

And what would happen when they returned to Boston?

Things were different in Boston.

Jack cradled his phone against his ear, staring out the window without seeing while he waited for the contracts department at Outland Systems to pick up on their end. He should be concentrating on the deal he needed to negotiate, but Emily filled his mind. He couldn't smell coffee without thinking of their morning-after bagels and coffee. He couldn't walk down the hall without glancing into her office.

And he sure as hell couldn't look Lloyd or Carmella in the eye. The wrap-up meeting he and Emily had with Lloyd late on Friday, a mere hour after their plane from Reno landed in Boston, had taken every ounce of his nerve. If Lloyd could read Emily as well as Emily claimed, would the older man sense that Jack had spent the night engaged in a tantalizing make-out session on the floor of Lloyd's own vacation home? Would he know Jack had awakened because he missed the heat of Emily's body beside him?

Thankfully, Jack recalled that Lloyd had kept the meeting brief so he could leave for a dinner meeting. But Jack and Emily had lingered in Lloyd's office, neither knowing what to say or do next, though Jack could sense Emily's relief at her father's quick exit.

He'd walked to the door, hoping to close it just enough to keep anyone from barreling in so he could ask Emily if she'd consider dating him—a real date, this time, with dinner and flowers and all the usual fanfare—when Carmella had approached from the other side, a copy of the week's financial reports ready for Lloyd's perusal.

Within seconds of striding past Jack, she realized Jack and Emily had been alone in the office and had flushed all the way to her newly darkened roots and backed out of the office. He'd cleared his throat and continued walking, trying to play off the awkward moment by thanking Carmella over his shoulder for taking such care with the arrangements for the trade show.

He wasn't sure she'd bought his casual act. If Lloyd didn't pester Emily for details of the trip to Reno, Carmella sure would. She was the mother hen of all mother hens. And she had to suspect what he now knew—that Lloyd had put them up in the house instead of in a hotel for the express purpose of getting the two of them together.

Or had Emily already spilled the beans? That would explain Carmella's instant embarrassment.

He fiddled with the pen on the corner of his desk. If only he knew where Emily's head was, now that she'd had a weekend away from him. Now that they were back on company turf, had she started thinking like a company girl again? If she was willing to tell Carmella about what had happened in Reno—any of what had happened in Reno—would she also feel obligated to tell her father about the financial indiscretions of one Patrick Devon? For years, he'd known that if the press caught wind of it, or if Lloyd discovered his secret through other means, Lloyd would feel betrayed that Jack hadn't told him first.

On the other hand, if he came clean with Lloyd, Jack risked losing the job that he'd worked so hard to attain—a position that had supported his mother until she'd remarried. Jack still helped pay for her condo, which she kept in her name, just so she'd never again be dependent on marriage for her financial well-being.

"Devon? You there?" The familiar voice of his counterpart at Outland Systems came over the line. "We gonna seal this deal, or what? We've got five million riding on getting this signed."

In other words, a ton of money. Riding on *him*. The gambler's son.

Jack yanked his gaze from the skyline and the view of the Quincy Shipyards back to his desk and the hallway beyond, where Emily sat not too far away. "Yep, but let me get a few things straight first."

"Oh, Emily," Carmella sighed as she closed the door to Emily's office behind her and approached the desk. "Something happened with you and Jack in Reno, didn't it? All our efforts, and your father succeeded anyway. Jack asked you out, didn't he? Your father goaded him into it, hoping he'd marry you someday."

Emily screwed up her mouth and rolled her eyes. "That's ridiculous, Carmella. Trust me, Jack Devon isn't the marrying type."

That's why things had been so different once they got back to Boston, from the second they stepped out of the cab at the Wintersoft offices—aka, the Real World—suitcases in tow, to meet with her father. That's why the sexual tension simmering between them changed from something exciting and tantalizing into a living, breathing monster.

Reno had been fun, at least while they enjoyed the privacy of the house. They could flirt, kiss—do whatever they wanted, really—and know it was casual.

Boston was work. Serious. Public. Very much like marriage.

Once that realization occurred to her, Jack's words came pounding back into her ears. On the rug, he'd told her in the same breath that he was very glad Lloyd had a daughter, but that he had *no intention of marrying into the company*. He'd even compared himself to Todd, saying he'd never do what Todd did.

She'd thought, at first, he'd meant he'd never abuse her trust as Todd had. But given what else he'd said at the house—that he wasn't the marrying type—perhaps he was giving her a gentle reminder that their romance was only temporary.

How could she have glossed over those words?

Because he's funny, intelligent, and movie-star handsome. And because he had you on your back in front of a roaring fire.

She let out a deep breath. She couldn't think about Jack, how he affected her simply by listening, by understanding—or about the fact that their fantasy time was at an end. She just had to chalk it up to a once-in-a-lifetime memory and move on. Just because he'd cleaned up the house the next morning and gotten breakfast started, and just because he'd treated her like a lady, didn't mean he wanted to keep her in his life. Not to date and definitely not to marry.

"But something did happen?" Carmella's eyes grew wide, and Emily started, wondering if Carmella could read her thoughts. "I knew it. I could tell from the way he looked at you, and you—"

"Carmella, it's not like that." The older woman was such a romantic, she'd probably decide what happened was a good thing. No way was Emily going to come clean with her.

"Then why did he stare at me like—" She clamped a hand to her mouth, then muttered, "Oh, no!"

Now it was Emily's turn to look alarmed. "What?"

"He knows! He knows about our matchmaking

plan, doesn't he? That you set up the other men, and that I helped you! That's why he looked at me that way. I knew it! I knew it the morning you had your meeting about the trip to Reno, and I dragged you into the ladies' room—''

''Don't worry, Carmella. Please.'' Carmella's hands started to shake, and Emily jumped up and guided her to a chair. ''He didn't know that morning. He suspected, but he didn't know. I told him.''

Disappointment and a sense of betrayal filled Carmella's soft eyes. ''Oh, Emily, dear. Why?''

''It's a long story. Let's just say he needed to know. But it's all right. He's not going to tell anyone.''

The older woman was no longer listening. ''Lloyd's going to hit the roof. He trusts me. Oh, Emily, there's so much you don't know. If your father discovers—''

''Carmella, Jack will *not* tell my father.''

Carmella took a ragged breath, then another one, before squaring her shoulders and standing, her face resolute. ''I suppose what's done is done. I'll just have to hope for the best.'' Her eyes focused on the clock near the door to Emily's office. ''Oh—the reason I originally came in here. Your father wants you to come to his office whenever you get the chance. We're planning to host a dinner party next week at his home and he'd like your input.''

Trying to lighten the mood, Emily said with a lilt, ''*We're* hosting a dinner party? Carmella...I never knew!''

The secretary flushed. "I meant that your father is hosting a dinner party. I'm merely making the arrangements."

"I know, Carmella, I just wanted to tease you. You will be there, though?"

"Of course."

"Good. Since I imagine most of the senior management will be invited—" A nod from Carmella confirmed her hypothesis. "Then you'll see for yourself that Jack can keep his mouth shut about the matchmaking plan."

"All right," Carmella groaned as she approached the door. "I suppose it is for the best. At least he knows what your father's up to, and he won't let Lloyd bully him into asking you out."

"See? All for the best," Emily agreed with a grin. "And could you close the door on your way out? Thanks."

Once Carmella was gone, Emily flipped the door's lock—thank goodness she'd had one installed so she'd feel more comfortable when working late—sat down behind her desk, then dropped her head into her hands for a good cry.

"I'm sorry. I didn't mean to interrupt. I can come back later." Emily took a step back, having barreled into her father's office without checking to be certain he was alone.

Of course, the other person in the room just had to be Jack. That's what she deserved for sitting in her office crying for who-knew-how-long, then wasting another half hour trying to calm down and messing with her compact to be sure her nose and eyes weren't red before heading to her dad's office, as he'd requested.

"No, we're about done, Emily," her father replied, gesturing to the chair beside Jack's. She eased into it, careful to keep her posture perfect so her feet wouldn't brush against Jack's in the narrow space between their chairs and her father's desk.

"We were finalizing a few things before our meeting with the investment bankers this morning," Jack explained, looking toward her without quite meeting her gaze. "But I think we're set."

Lloyd nodded. "And I invited Jack to a dinner party at the house this Friday." He glanced over his papers toward Jack.

"You can attend?"

"Of course." Jack replied before Lloyd turned his focus to Emily.

"The guest list is currently sitting around forty, so this will be a larger affair than usual. I was hoping you could look over the catering details with Carmella. She does a wonderful job, but for this occasion, I'd like a little something extra."

Emily raised an eyebrow. "And what is the occasion?" Her father was known for his frequent dinner parties, but they were usually limited to ten or twelve guests—not forty. "Business or pleasure?"

"A little of both. Mostly pleasure. But that's all I'm saying for now."

Emily shook her head at the mischievous gleam in

her father's clear blue eyes. He loved to surprise people, and she had no doubt something unusual would happen at the party.

She shifted in her chair. She hated to mention it in front of Jack, but she had no choice. "I'm happy to help Carmella with the plans, but I may be late to arrive on Friday."

"I don't want you to miss this. Is it important?"

She swallowed, unable to look at Jack as she spoke. "That's the day Randall Wellingby will be here from ABG, and I've already promised to meet with him that evening. I hope he'll have some good news for us."

Her father perked up. "Really? Then please, bring him to the party. I'll have Carmella add his name to the guest list. I'd like to meet him myself, if he's going to be a client."

At that exact moment, Carmella stuck her head in the door. "The investment bankers are waiting for you in the lobby," she said to Lloyd. "I have coffee and Danish set up in the conference room, so you can greet them and escort them in any time."

Lloyd thanked Carmella as he grabbed his materials for the meeting and strode out the door. Over his shoulder, he said, "See you in there, Jack."

Emily stood and looked to Jack, who was gathering his own papers for the meeting and shoving them into a file. "Jack?"

He glanced up at her, his eyes hooded, unreadable. "Yeah?"

"Well, what do you think?" She shouldn't ask, but

she wanted to make one last attempt to discover the truth about his feelings, for the sake of her heart.

"I'm prepared. I think the investment bankers are going to be thrilled with—"

She let out a noisy breath. "I'm referring to taking Randall to my father's dinner party, and you know it. What are your thoughts? Do *you* think I should bring him?" As much as she knew she didn't need to ask his permission, and as much sense as it made for her to take Randall, since he'd likely be the liaison between ABG and Wintersoft in their future dealings, she wanted Jack to tell her not to. To tell her he'd hoped to spend the evening with her himself.

He shrugged and pushed the last of the papers into the file folder.

"Jack?"

"I'm sure it'll be a great opportunity for Randall to get to know Wintersoft better."

"That's not what I—" Without looking at her, he rose from his chair and was gone, making his way down the hall to his meeting. She'd wanted to say, *that's not what I meant. I meant given what happened with us.*

Not a word had been spoken about their time in Reno since they'd returned to Boston. But apparently, there was no *us*. Not in Jack's mind.

She bit back a sigh and put both her hands to her head, lacing her fingers through her hair, trying to get control of herself. Jack might have realized he didn't possess his father's gambling tendencies, but as much as he cared about her and desired her—at least during their time in Reno, and as he'd admitted, for months, if not years, before that—he hadn't gotten past his parents' failed marriage. Or realized his future relationships wouldn't be dictated by theirs the way she'd finally realized that she wasn't bound by what had happened between her and Todd.

She muttered an uncharacteristic expletive, then reached across her father's desk for his phone and dialed into her voice mail, scribbling down Randall's New York phone number when the system got to his message.

Clearly Jack still wasn't the marrying type. No matter. She was the dedicated-to-the-company type, and that meant Randall would be her date for the dinner party. And she wouldn't feel one ounce of guilt about it. This was business, pure and simple. Which was apparently the way Jack now wanted things, too.

Chapter Ten

The moment Emily punched the play button on her home answering machine, she knew she'd made a mistake.

She'd inserted the key in the door of her Beacon Hill apartment just as the nearby Cheers bar was locking its doors for the night, only a block away on the edge of the Boston Public Garden. After agonizing about Jack half the day, she'd been compelled to burn the midnight oil trying to return e-mails she'd put off during her trip to Reno, as well as catching up on work she'd allowed to stagnate while she'd been distracted.

After spending the last five hours alone in the Wintersoft offices—save for the late-night janitor—her heart had soared when she'd walked into her darkened apartment to see the blinking light on the machine. Someone had thought of her.

Maybe Jack had called to apologize?

He'd left the office soon after his meeting with the investment bankers, cutting off any chance she had to continue their conversation. Still, she knew that as much as she wanted to see him, to talk to him about what had happened in Reno and how they'd handle it in the office, that he needed to approach her first.

"Please, please, let it be Jack," she murmured as she hit the button.

But the male voice on the machine had a thick British accent. "Emily! Thanks for calling me back this afternoon—it was wonderful to phone in for my messages and hear your voice instead of my highly aggravated accountant's."

Oh, no. Way too exuberant.

"I hate that we're doing all this by voice mail, which is why I thought I'd try you at home. I just wanted to let you know that I'd enjoy attending your father's dinner party. Of course, I'd hoped we could go out to dinner on our own, as I believe we'll have a new partnership to celebrate. But I'll be in Boston all weekend, so perhaps we can arrange something on our own on Saturday? Though I do look forward to meeting your father, of course."

A date. He wanted a date. This time, she couldn't just chalk his words up to a case of innocent flirting. She closed her eyes as the end of the message played.

"Give me a call and we can chat. You have my number in New York."

In other words, he needed to know where she stood.

She opened her eyes and erased the message, then slid out of her jacket and tossed it over one of the barstools lining the granite-topped peninsula separating her living room from her tiny kitchen.

The digital clock on her over-the-range microwave read 2:10 a.m. She'd missed dinner, but didn't have the energy to cook.

"Years without any dates except those my father foisted on me, and now two men to deal with at once," she grumbled aloud as she reached into the fridge and pulled out a bowl of cold pasta shells. One man who wanted her; one whom she wanted with all her heart and soul.

She leaned a hip against one of the barstools and began opening her mail as she used her other hand to pop the shells into her mouth, not bothering with a fork.

The mail, unfortunately, wasn't enough of a distraction. She pushed it aside and finished the pasta, wiped her hands on a paper towel, then shuffled toward her bedroom, kicking her shoes off in the living room on the way.

Asking Randall to the dinner party had been a mistake. She'd given him the wrong impression by inviting him to something as personal as a dinner at her father's home, even if there were forty other guests, and her father had urged her to do so.

Randall now believed she was interested. Just as she'd thought Jack was interested in her. And true, she did find Randall attractive. Tall, lean, blond, polite—and that accent!—what wasn't to like? But after the last week, she knew her heart belonged to Jack, whether she wanted it to or not. And whether he wanted it or not.

But what could she do?

Jack hesitated on the sidewalk outside Lloyd Winters's restored brownstone in the Back Bay. The residence was situated a few steps back from the sidewalk on a well-known street which backed onto the Esplanade and the Charles River, just a couple blocks from the ritz and glitz of Newbury Street shopping, and a short walk from the peaceful, meandering sidewalks that cut through the Boston Public Garden. A dusting of snow covered the small landscaped area between the sidewalk and the building, and above him, he could hear laughter and the excited chatter of party guests, even though the home's tall windows were closed to the chilly February air.

Lloyd's dinner party ranked as one of *the* places to be in Boston tonight, judging from the guest list Jack glimpsed on Carmella's desk. Nearly all the upper-level management from Wintersoft would be here, along with several of Lloyd's longtime friends and business contacts—a who's who list of Boston's software industry—and a few social mavens, to boot. But Jack couldn't conjure up the excitement he usually felt when invited to attend an event at Lloyd's home, which occupied the top two floors of the brownstone.

This time, he wouldn't be angling to network with a potential client or to introduce himself to members of Boston's upper crust, in the hope of making future connections for the company. Lloyd made it clear the evening was for pleasure.

And Emily would be here on Randall Wellingby's arm, instead of his.

Jack's gut twisted at the image of her looking up into Randall's blue eyes, laughing at his dry British humor, giving Randall the smile Jack desperately wanted for himself. He shouldn't have blown her off this afternoon. And he should have ignored Carmella, and just cleared things up with Emily last Friday, when they'd arrived back in Boston. This past week, since they'd left Reno, had been the longest and most agonizing of his life, as he and Emily passed by each other dozens of times in the office halls, with hardly a word being exchanged. More than once, he'd wanted to stop her, to pull her into an office and tell her how badly he wanted her.

But were the feelings mutual? If so, then how could she bring Randall tonight, after what happened in Reno?

Because you didn't tell her that you've fallen for her, you idiot.

He swallowed hard, then shrugged, adjusting his double-breasted, long wool jacket across his shoulders. He'd just have to face them. He had no choice. Even if he had told her how he felt, she probably wouldn't have agreed to date him. They shared a connection that bordered on the cosmic—and he knew she'd felt it, too—but her experience with Todd meant she'd probably run as far and as fast as possible if he told her he loved her. She didn't want an office romance.

And—his difficulty at facing Emily tonight aside—he'd have to hope this wasn't the last party he'd attend at Lloyd's. If Emily fell for Randall, then between her allegiance to her father and her lack of romantic interest in him, there would be little to prevent her from telling her father everything about his past.

Still, relationship-preventing or not, career-busting or not, he couldn't bring himself to regret telling her. His secret was finally out. Until the moment he'd described his father's descent into addiction, how painful it had been for him and his mother, he'd never comprehended how heavy a burden he'd carried. Emily had understood. She'd listened without judgment, and without pity. She'd also understood Jack's fear that he, too, might harbor the same obsessive drive.

But that had been in Reno.

"Jack!" A distinctive male voice shouted from a few doors away. "Not lost, are you?"

Jack turned to see Matt Burke, Wintersoft's Senior Vice President of Accounting, with his arm resting protectively around the shoulders of his new wife, Sarah.

Jack forced a warm grin to his face, even as a wave of envy buffeted him. Sarah worked as Matt's secretary for years, and they'd been tiptoeing around their attraction to each other the entire time. But last fall, they'd decided to get married. No one who saw them look at each other could mistake the happiness they shared.

The kind of happiness he'd blown with Emily.

For a moment, he imagined what it would be like if he could propose to her, if they could share what Matt and Sarah shared.

He turned his face to the starlit sky, and he could swear he heard Emily's laughter floating down from the party upstairs.

It figured. Matt's file was one of those she and Carmella had accessed. This marriage was partially Emily's doing.

In order to *prevent* an office marriage for herself.

"It's been a while, and all these brownstones look the same in the winter," Jack finally replied, turning back to Matt and Sarah as the couple approached Lloyd's front door. "I was just double-checking before I walked inside."

"Well, Lloyd tells me he has something special planned tonight, and I don't want to miss it." The edge of Sarah's mouth curved up as she strode ahead of the men to reach for the large iron-and-glass door to the lobby of Lloyd's brownstone, where a uniformed man stood waiting to take their coats and direct them to the elevator.

"Any idea what it could be?" Matt asked as they stepped into the tiny, marble-walled lift.

"Haven't really thought about it." His mind had been fixed on Emily. "But I'm sure Lloyd will tell us all soon enough."

When the elevator opened into Lloyd's foyer on

the fourth floor, Jack held back, allowing Matt and Sarah to step out first.

As he expected, they were immediately swamped by several other couples from Wintersoft. Grant Lawson and his wife, Ariana, whom Emily had helped through the last days of her pregnancy, approached Matt and Sarah first, and the foursome quickly began chatting about Ariana's newborn twins. Nate Leeman and Kate Sanderson, who were engaged to be married, stood nearby with Brett and Sunny Hamilton, and Jack couldn't help but notice the discreet smile that passed between Brett and Sunny at Ariana's talk of children. Reed Connors and his new wife, Samantha, waved from the back of the room, and as they made their way through the crowd toward Matt and Sarah, Jack slipped behind the smiling couples and made his way toward the kitchen. Their communal happiness only heightened his own sense of love lost, and he figured a drink or a cup of coffee might calm him before he had to face Emily and Randall.

He caught a whiff of brewing coffee, and turned the corner into the kitchen, only to come face to face with Lloyd and Carmella, who each seemed even happier than the couples by the front door.

Worse, Emily stood right behind them. And she was wearing a drop dead gorgeous red dress, one that plunged at the neckline and hugged her hips to accentuate every delicious curve of her body.

This had to be every man's nightmare.

He forced his gaze to her father. "Lloyd, thanks for inviting me. It's great to be here," he added, though he wished he could be anywhere else. If he'd been compelled to socialize with Emily and her date at a dinner party tonight hosted by anyone other than his boss, he'd have made the excuse that he needed to work late.

"Glad you could make it, Jack. You know my home is open to you anytime." Lloyd's voice was welcoming as he clapped a hand onto Jack's shoulder. "Grab a drink, enjoy yourself."

"Thanks, I will." But before the words were out of his mouth, Jack noticed Emily cringe. It was only a split-second look—while Emily's gaze traveled to her father's hand, which still rested on Jack's shoulder—but in that instant, for the first time, Jack understood how much it pained Emily that her father treated him like a son.

The same way Lloyd treated Todd. And apparently didn't treat her.

Lloyd took his hand from Jack's shoulder and poured himself a Scotch. He looked past Jack toward the crowd filling his opulent living and dining rooms. "You know, Jack, I think this is going to be my best dinner party ever. All the people who are important to me were able to make it." He frowned for a second, scanning the faces. "You know, it's odd. Six months ago, most of these couples weren't married. Weren't even together. I never realized it before, but all of the single men on the Wintersoft senior management team have been married this past year. Well, except you. Don't you find that unusual?"

Jack stole a glance at Emily, and the panic in her

eyes made his chest heavy. No wonder Emily felt compelled to circumvent her father and find girl-friends for his staff. Lloyd was all too aware of their personal relationships.

He fixed his gaze on Lloyd. Whether he got fired or not, Jack knew he had to tell Lloyd the truth, if only to save Emily from her father's matchmaking and allow her to prove to him that she could do quite well without marrying anyone at the company.

"Well, there's a reason I'm not married, Lloyd," Jack began, making sure he had the older man's un-divided attention. "It's something I've avoided telling you for quite some time, but I believe you should know, because it can affect the company—"

"Dad, can you help me out here?" Emily inter-rupted, opening the refrigerator door and waving her father over. "It's important."

"Oh, Em, just have the caterer help you—"

"Dad. Please."

Jack looked from Emily to Lloyd. He didn't know what Emily wanted to say, but clearly she didn't want her father to discover the truth about Patrick Devon. His admiration for her kicked up another notch, at the same time, guilt struck him at how easily he'd be-lieved she'd betray his trust.

She never would have told her father.

"Dad?" Emily's voice was firmer this time.

Jack ran a hand over his chin. He couldn't possibly barrel on without being rude, but there was no way he'd allow Emily to continue on as the object of her father's matchmaking schemes. And once he was gone—either fired, or at least ruled out as an accept-able husband—Em would be off the hook.

"Why don't you help your daughter," he said. Then, with a pointed glance at Emily, he added, "I promise, Lloyd, I'll fill you in as soon as you're free."

Emily shot him a look that said, don't you dare, but Jack pretended not to see and wandered toward the living room.

It was only after he'd been talking to Brett and Sunny for a few minutes that Jack realized one guest was conspicuously absent.

Randall Wellingby.

"What's going on, Emily?"

Em summoned up her courage as her father stood in his library staring at her, Scotch in hand, wrinkles of concern furrowing his brow.

"We need to talk, Dad."

One side of his mouth quirked up. "In the middle of my dinner party?"

Pushing forward, Emily began, "I know you like Jack Devon a great deal."

"What's not to like? The man's a workhorse. Mo-ral, good-looking, and intelligent. I trust his judgment. He's like a son to me."

"That's the thing, Dad," Emily forced herself not to let her anger seep into her voice. "He's like a son to you. Todd was like a son to you. But you don't afford me the same level of respect."

Lloyd's frown returned, and he set his Scotch down

on one of the library's mahogany end tables, then took a seat in the leather chair beside it. "Emily, you're my daughter, and I love you. You know that. What's gotten into you?"

"You said yourself that you trust Jack's judgment. Yet you don't trust mine. I know you love me, but you're old-fashioned. You think I can't exercise independent thought or something—well, I don't know exactly what you think—but it's certain that you don't afford me the same level of respect you do the men in the company."

"Emily, you're my Vice President of Global Sales. You've earned that position, the same as any VP would—"

"I know that. But this isn't about responsibility." She puffed out a breath, letting her frustration get the better of her. "Dad, why are you so intent on marrying me off to someone in the company? Again? I've tried and tried to convince you not to, but even after the disaster in my first marriage, you won't stop!"

"What makes you think I have any plans—"

"I found out." She held up a hand and added, "And don't ask me how. You were going to urge some of the senior management to ask me out. Lucky for me, they're all married now. Or mostly." With the notable exception of Jack.

"You're right," Lloyd leaned farther back in the chair, resigned to admit to the truth. "But it's not, I repeat, *not*, because I don't respect you or your judgment, Emily. Or because I think you need a man to take care of you. You do an admirable job all on your own.'' He took a sip of his Scotch, then added, ''The fact I want you to have a man in your life doesn't mean your mother and I would have preferred a son to you. I wouldn't trade you—exactly the way you are—for anything in the world, sweetheart. It might sound corny, but you're my proudest accomplishment.''

Emily sighed. She loved him so much, but he could be so frustrating. ''Then why are you doing this, Dad? I don't need you to be my dating service. And that's just what you were about to do in the kitchen with Jack, when you pointed out that he was single. Weren't you?''

''I just want you to be happy, Em. I know you've always wanted children, and you know what difficulty your mother and I had.'' Even as he said it, Emily could see the pain all the years of trying to conceive—and failing—had on her parents. ''I never, ever want that frustration for you. And you know, as you get older, it gets more difficult—''

Not wanting to get into a discussion about her biological clock with her father, Emily interrupted, ''But that doesn't explain why you want me to marry someone at Wintersoft.''

''Because I know they'd understand you. Take Jack Devon, for instance—''

''I'd rather not.'' Well, she would. If he was the kind of guy who believed in marriage, love and happily-ever-afters.

''Humor me. I'm being hypothetical here. Jack values the company as much as you do. He's wrapped his life up in it. I know you—even after you have children, you'll want to continue working in some capacity. Who would better understand your dedication to the company than someone who already works there?''

''Todd didn't,'' she pointed out. He wanted to be married to the boss's daughter. He didn't care about her, not apart from the benefits she represented to his career.

''That was Todd. I misjudged him. But I don't think I'm misjudging Jack. Or that I misjudged any of the other men at the company when I decided to ask them to consider taking you out—though I never got the chance.''

''Just let me do it on my own, okay?'' She crossed the library and took her father's hands. ''Please?''

''But—''

''Have you ever considered that those men out there married who they did for a reason? That maybe there's a right person for everyone, and that they have to find that person themselves?''

Even though she'd pushed some of the newlyweds attending the dinner party in the right direction, none of the couples would have married if they hadn't loved each other, and if they hadn't taken the steps necessary to discern that fact for themselves.

''I think,'' she said slowly, making sure her father was getting each and every word, ''that even when a person is right under your nose, and you see them every day, and even if they're the perfect person for you, it can take years for a romantic relationship to develop. It has to be handled carefully. And it can't be pushed by outside forces.''

Noise from the party filtered down the hall to them, and a slow smile spread across her father's face. "You know, when you put it that way, I have to agree."

He stood and gave her a bear hug. "Oh, Emily, believe me, I agree, never more so than tonight. Listen, if I ever, ever made you feel that I didn't love you with all my heart, or that I would have preferred a son to you, I'm sorry. And I promise, from now on, no interference."

"Thanks, Dad." A wave of relief swept through her as she hugged her father back. "And if I jumped to conclusions, I'm sorry, too. I know you only want what's best for me."

"Though I really think Jack Devon—"

She stepped back and frowned at him, despite his teasing tone. This was too easy. After years of asking him not to interfere, he was going to actually leave her love life alone?

"I promise!" he held up a hand and laughed. "You don't have to worry about me. You'll understand later tonight. I told you I have a surprise for you."

Before she could pester him into elaborating further, he guided her out of the library. "Let's not leave our guests unattended any longer."

As they entered the living room once more, however, a firm hand gripped Emily's elbow. "Follow me."

Chapter Eleven

Jack steered Emily though the crowd, stopping to say hello to colleagues and other guests as they went, but never relaxing his casual-yet-determined grip on her elbow as he steered her toward the back of the living room and the tiny hallway that housed the back stairs.

"What?" she hissed, unwilling to let anyone see that Jack was trying to get her alone.

He ignored her, and when no one was looking, he pulled her into the hall and up the staircase to the brownstone's top floor. He turned her to the right, and through the door to her father's glass-walled conservatory, which offered a rooftop view of the Charles River and the Esplanade. Her father frequently entertained guests here in the summer, and Jack had spent more than one Fourth of July party here, watching as the Boston Pops played the "1812 Overture" and fireworks exploded over the Charles to celebrate the holiday. Now, however, in the dead of winter, the cushions had been removed from the wicker furniture and the plant racks stood empty, the ferns and violets having been moved to the warmer lower floor.

"I'm sorry to yank you out of the party, Emily, but," Jack turned and faced her, determination in his eyes. "We've got to talk."

"You don't need to tell my father about your dad," Emily replied, hoping she sounded more comfortable being alone with Jack in the confines of the quiet conservatory than she felt. "That's what you were going to tell him in the kitchen, wasn't it? Why?"

"I have my reasons." Deep furrows crossed his brow as he spoke. "One, I feel dishonest keeping it from him. If it's ever discovered, it'd be his reputation at stake, too. He doesn't need a newspaper suddenly revealing that one of his executives, one who juggles millions and millions of dollars for him every day, has a family history of gambling addiction."

"It's not a history. It's one person. He's dead, and you're not like him." She put a tentative hand on his arm. "Look, Jack, if you feel that strongly about telling him, I can't stop you. But my guess is that he won't care. You've told me, and I don't think there's any risk to the company or to my father."

He let out an exasperated breath and, shaking off her hand, took a few steps away from her to stand by the windows. "It's more than that, Emily."

"Then what? What other reason could you possibly have?"

"Look, it's between me and your father." He kept

his eyes riveted on the Charles River, flowing wide and black below them in the February night. The yellow lights of Cambridge and MIT glowed on the river's far side, providing the room's only illumination. "I didn't bring you up here to discuss your father, or mine. I need to find out—"

"No," she said, cutting him off. "Let's finish talking about this, first, because things are getting clearer for me now."

He shot her a dismissive look, but it didn't work. "You think that if you tell my father about your family history, he won't try to push you into asking me out. You know how much I hate his interference in my love life, and since you're the only single male left in all of upper management, you figure that by confessing your secret to my dad, he'll deem you unworthy of his little girl. And he'll stop trying to play Cupid for me."

"You're reading things into this."

"I don't think so. That's why you brought it up when you did. In the kitchen. He was talking about how many couples had gotten married in the last year, but pointed out that you were still single." She walked across the room's tiled floor and past the wicker coffee table and chairs to stand by Jack's side at the window. She could tell from the look on his face that her theory was correct.

She flashed him a grin she hoped would ease the strain evident on his face. "I know part of me should be offended, but you know, that was sweet. Thank you."

"I wasn't trying to be heroic, you know. I was planning to tell him anyway." He shrugged, then tilted his head to meet her gaze. "I just figured that since you'd brought Randall, it was for the best to tell your father right away. To keep him off your back."

"I didn't bring Randall."

"Yeah, I figured that out after you disappeared with your father."

He shoved his hands in the pockets of his tailored black slacks as he spoke, and once again, Emily found it hard to breathe as he looked at her. The man was just devastatingly handsome. The semi-darkness of the room only served to emphasize the planes of his face and the endless depth of his eyes.

How could she ever look at him and not picture the evening they'd spent curled in front of the fireplace? How could she ever not love him?

"Jack," she chose her words deliberately, "was Randall the only reason you tried to stop my father from playing matchmaker?"

"I'll tell you if you tell me why you didn't bring him to the party." He took a step toward her, his hands still firmly in his pockets. "Grant Lawson tells me that as of this evening, ABG is officially Wintersoft's newest client. He got a call from you this afternoon to draw up the legal paperwork."

"That's true." She couldn't help but be proud of the accomplishment. "Our demonstration at the trade show, together with the materials we provided Randall, gave him enough ammunition to convince the

ABG board to dump Acton and come over to Wintersoft.''

"Good for you.'' Jack's smile went all the way to his eyes, making his appreciation of her skill and hard work clear.

"Thanks.''

"So why didn't you bring him?''

Emily studied Jack's face, wondering how much she dared to say. "I knew he'd appreciate being invited, but it didn't feel right.''

"Even though your father urged you to bring him?''

She shook her head. "It wasn't right. Randall's a wonderful guy, and as a new client, I know he'd love to be here. But I think you were correct when you said that he might be attracted to me. So I cancelled on him and told him I'd just meet him in New York next week. At his office, not out for dinner. I didn't want to lead him on, and...'' She shrugged. "I just didn't want to lead him on.''

Jack's hands slipped out of his pockets, and he curled them around the tops of her bare arms. "I want to know the 'and,' Emily. The other reason you didn't think it was right.''

Now or never. She closed her eyes for a moment, gathering her wits, then met Jack's gaze. "And, if you have to know the truth, I didn't want Randall to feel as rotten as I've felt this last week. I didn't want him to fall for me the way I've fallen for you, knowing nothing can ever come of it.''

Jack slid one of his hands from her arm up to her

nape, then gradually to her cheek. "You've fallen for me?"

Her chest felt as though she lay beneath a pile of bricks, but she gave a slight nod, just enough so he could feel the movement against his palm.

"Good," he whispered. "Because this last week was the most miserable of my life, too."

Before Emily could react, Jack's lips were on hers, giving her the most gentle, sweet kiss she'd ever experienced in her life.

"I'm in love with you, Emily," he said, cupping her face between his palms. "I've been attracted to you for years, but on the inside, I've made excuse after excuse to keep from falling for you. My father's addiction, my parents' horrible marriage—I even tried to convince myself this week that our time in Reno probably meant nothing to you, and that the first thing you'd do when you got back was to tell your father about my family. But, of course, you didn't. It's not who you are."

He allowed his gaze to wander over her, from her neat, upswept hair to her red dress, then finally back to her face. His eyes sparkled with adoration as he said, "You're one of a kind, Emily Winters. You're intelligent, you're beautiful, and you care about those around you more than you're willing to admit. You might have thought your matchmaking scheme was solely to defend yourself from your father, but I know better. I watched you go out of your way to make the people in your life happy. To give them a chance at the happiness you believed you'd never have after your marriage to Todd didn't work out. But you can be happy, Em. You can. With me.''

Her eyes burned with tears, but she tried to keep them in check as she smiled at Jack. ''You, the man known around the office as *Boston Magazine*'s Hottest Bachelor, are in love with *me?* You know I'm not the partying type.''

He laughed aloud. ''Me, neither. Never have been. You want to know the dirty secret behind that article?''

At her raised eyebrow, he explained. ''A friend of mine from college wrote that article after he saw me out on dates with two different women in the same week and made assumptions. Wrong assumptions. I think he believed he was doing me a favor—making me look like a playboy type so I could score even more dates.''

''And you're saying this wasn't a favor?''

He shook his head, then kissed her again, and Emily savored the slow, deliberate movement of his mouth on hers and the feel of his strong hands caressing her back.

''Actually,'' he added, pulling her close and keeping his voice low and intimate, ''I've always wanted what I never had growing up. A loving, stable home life. Like yours with your parents. To me, that sounds like heaven. And I've never felt it more possible than I do with you.''

The noise of the party floated up the stairs to them as someone switched the music in her father's stereo system from classical to a thrumming, party-atmosphere nuevo flamenco and cranked up the volume.

She glanced at the conservatory door. All her colleagues were just a few steps away, past those doors. People who'd pry into her life, who might question whether her relationship with Jack would turn out as her marriage to Todd had. She knew it never could— Jack and Todd came from opposite ends of the spectrum, personality- and morality-wise. But still.

She turned her eyes back to Jack, and saw that he, also, had been looking at the door. "It's going to be very, very difficult to date while we work together. After what happened with Todd, I don't know if I can…"

She put a tentative hand on his chest, and his heart melted beneath her tiny palm as she turned her sapphire eyes up to his. "But I can't be without you, either."

"Then let's not date." Jack put his hand over hers, wanting more than anything to have her with him forever, to know he'd wake up each morning beside her, able to touch her and make love to her. To share a morning paper with her, to share a family with her. "Let's get married."

"What?" Her mouth opened in astonishment, then her lower lips began to shake, nearly sending him over the edge. "Isn't this a bit…a bit sudden?"

"I can wait, if I have to. But, Em, I know in my heart that no other woman will ever understand me the way you do. No other woman will intrigue me or challenge me, or, truth be told," he gave her a wicked grin as he finished, "turn me on the way you do. And I know, as certainly as any man can, that will be true for the rest of my life."

"You told me you weren't the marrying type." Her voice sounded firm, despite her trembling jaw, and he knew he had to give the right answer, or lose her right there.

"Until this week, I didn't think I was."

He sucked in a deep breath, willing his heart to slow so Emily wouldn't feel it pounding beneath her fingertips and mistake his excitement for doubt. Every doubt he'd ever had had left him during those moments he'd stood outside her father's brownstone, waiting to come inside, knowing Randall would have his arm around the only woman he'd even considered marriage material.

"You showed me the possibilities, Emily. I know I could never love anything—gambling, or my own career ambitions—or anyone more than I love you. I suspected it in Reno, when I woke up in front of the fireplace and ached because you weren't there. And I knew it for certain when we got back to Boston. I didn't want to work. I only wanted to be with you and to make you happy. And I want to be with you for the rest of my life."

Still holding her hand to his chest, Jack sank to one knee on the tile floor. His heart felt as if it would explode from his chest as he gazed at the only woman he could ever love with all his soul. "Marry me, Emily."

She frowned at him, but her eyes held a smile.

"How long an engagement would you want? Hypothetically speaking, of course."

He grinned up at her. "As long as you like."

"Would a week do? I could probably stretch it out to a month—"

Before she could finish, he pulled her down to him and kissed her. He could hardly believe it, and he knew the ear-to-ear smile plastering his face showed his pleasure. "That soon?"

"I was kidding, actually. You know my father—and probably Carmella—would want to be involved in planning something wild and splashy and totally inappropriate."

He laughed, knowing her words were all too true.

She ran a finger over his chin, and the gentle smile on her face filled his heart with joy. "But whether it's a week from now or a year from now, I would love to marry you, Jack Devon. Nothing would make me happier."

"Does my hair look okay?" Emily asked as she and Jack stood at the bottom of the stairs, in the hallway just outside the now-boisterous living and dining rooms.

"Well, you're a little flushed." His eyes held a devious gleam as he smoothed the back of her red dress and added, "But you look beautiful. And if someone suspects what we've been up to for the last half hour or so, do we really care?"

One side of her mouth jerked up at Jack. Her *fiancé*. "No, I suppose we don't. We'd better hurry though—it sounds like they're sitting down to dinner."

"There you two are," Lloyd laughed as Jack and Emily grabbed the last two available chairs. Two tables had been set up in the long dining room, each set for twenty. "Now, I propose a toast. I invited all of you here tonight for a very specific reason. To celebrate an engagement."

Emily gasped aloud, and Jack instantly colored.

Then Carmella shrieked, "I knew it! You two *are* together!"

Every eye in the room turned to Jack and Emily.

"Never seen you blush before, Devon, so I'll take that as an affirmative," Lloyd laughed. "And we'll discuss this later, Emily."

The entire room erupted into a cacophony of whistles and cheers. After a few moments, Lloyd called for quiet. "As you can see, this comes as a complete surprise to me."

"Then whose engagement are we celebrating?" Brett Hamilton asked, glancing from Jack and Emily to Lloyd.

"Mine," he grinned. "You are all cordially invited to my wedding this summer, when, in this very house, I will marry Carmella Lopez."

"No way," Emily whispered to herself. Tears obscured her vision as she raced around the table to hug first her father, then Carmella. "No way!"

"I take it this is good news, Emily?" Carmella asked, hesitation in her voice.

"Carmella, I think this is the best match you've

ever made,'' she laughed. ''Well, with one notable exception.''

''And I told you,'' Lloyd cut in, ''that you should marry a man like Jack Devon.''

Emily turned to see Jack standing beside her, and the look of happiness in his eyes sent tears spilling onto her cheeks.

As she clasped Jack's free hand, her father raised his glass. ''To Wintersoft, and to each and every one of the fabulous employees in this room,'' he toasted. ''We are more than a company. We're a family. And like a family, I hope we continue to find success, happiness and love.''

As Jack leaned down and kissed her, Emily heard forty voices cheer together, ''And love!''

*　*　*　*　*

SILHOUETTE *Romance*®

**Discover what happens
when wishes come true
in**

**A brand-new miniseries
from reader favorite**

Teresa Southwick

*Three friends, three birthdays,
three loves of a lifetime!*

BABY, OH BABY!
(Silhouette Romance #1704, Available January 2004)

FLIRTING WITH THE BOSS
(Silhouette Romance #1708, Available February 2004)

AN HEIRESS ON HIS DOORSTEP
(Silhouette Romance #1712, Available March 2004)

Available at your favorite retail outlet.

Visit Silhouette at www.eHarlequin.com   SRIWW

SILHOUETTE *Romance*®

Marrying The Boss's Daughter

Who will marry the boss's daughter?

Wintersoft's CEO is on a husband hunt for his daughter. Trouble is Emily has uncovered his scheme. Can she marry off the eligible executives in the company before Dad sets his crazy plan in motion?

Love, Your Secret Admirer by SUSAN MEIER
(on sale September 2003)

Her Pregnant Agenda by LINDA GOODNIGHT
(on sale October 2003)

Fill-in Fiancée by DeANNA TALCOTT
(on sale November 2003)

Santa Brought a Son by MELISSA McCLONE
(on sale December 2003)

Rules of Engagement by CARLA CASSIDY
(on sale January 2004)

One Bachelor To Go by NICOLE BURNHAM
(on sale February 2004)

With office matchmakers on the loose, is any eligible executive safe?

Available at your favorite retail outlet.

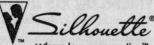

Silhouette®
Where love comes alive™

Visit Silhouette at www.eHarlequin.com

SRMTBD

SILHOUETTE *Romance* ®

presents

THE SECRET PRINCESS
by Elizabeth Harbison
(Silhouette Romance #1713)

**Once small-town bookseller Amy Scott had completed
her transformation from plain Jane to regal princess,
would she still need her handsome royal tutor?**

Available March 2004 at your favorite retail outlet.

Visit Silhouette at www.eHarlequin.com   SRTSP

SILHOUETTE *Romance*®

presents

MAJOR DADDY
by Cara Colter
(Silhouette Romance #1710)

When Major Cole Standen retired, he figured he'd quit
the rescuing business for good. Then five irresistible
tykes—and their sweet and sexy auntie Brooke—
turned up on his doorstep, desperate for his help.
Now, knee-deep in diapers and baby bottles, the
major was suddenly picturing himself with a brood
of his own...and beautiful Brooke as his bride!

Available March 2004 at your favorite retail outlet.

Visit Silhouette at www.eHarlequin.com   SRMD

If you enjoyed what you just read,
then we've got an offer you can't resist!

Take 2 bestselling
love stories FREE!
Plus get a FREE surprise gift!

Clip this page and mail it to Silhouette Reader Service

IN U.S.A.
3010 Walden Ave.
P.O. Box 1867
Buffalo, N.Y. 14240-1867

IN CANADA
P.O. Box 609
Fort Erie, Ontario
L2A 5X3

YES! Please send me 2 free Silhouette Romance® novels and my free surprise gift. After receiving them, if I don't wish to receive anymore, I can return the shipping statement marked cancel. If I don't cancel, I will receive 6 brand-new novels every month, before they're available in stores! In the U.S.A., bill me at the bargain price of $21.34 per shipment plus 25¢ shipping and handling per book and applicable sales tax, if any*. In Canada, bill me at the bargain price of $24.68 plus 25¢ shipping and handling per book and applicable taxes**. That's the complete price and a savings of at least 10% off the cover prices—what a great deal! I understand that accepting the 2 free books and gift places me under no obligation ever to buy any books. I can always return a shipment and cancel at any time. Even if I never buy another book from Silhouette, the 2 free books and gift are mine to keep forever.

209 SDN DU9H
309 SDN DU9J

Name _____ (PLEASE PRINT)

Address _____ Apt.# _____

City _____ State/Prov. _____ Zip/Postal Code _____

* Terms and prices subject to change without notice. Sales tax applicable in N.Y.
** Canadian residents will be charged applicable provincial taxes and GST.
   All orders subject to approval. Offer limited to one per household and not valid to
   current Silhouette Romance® subscribers.
   ® are registered trademarks of Harlequin Books S.A., used under license.

SROM03   ©1998 Harlequin Enterprises Limited

eHARLEQUIN.com

For **FREE online reading,** visit
www.eHarlequin.com now and enjoy:

Online Reads
Read **Daily** and **Weekly** chapters from
our Internet-exclusive stories by your
favorite authors.

Red-Hot Reads
Turn up the heat with one of our more
sensual online stories!

Interactive Novels
Cast your vote to help decide how these
stories unfold...then stay tuned!

Quick Reads
For shorter romantic reads, try our
collection of Poems, Toasts, & More!

Online Read Library
Miss one of our online reads?
Come here to catch up!

Reading Groups
Discuss, share and rave with other
community members!

**For great reading online,
visit www.eHarlequin.com today!**

INTONL

Wedding rings were bought.

Passionate kisses shared.

But neither the bride nor groom planned on falling in love as part of their marriage bargain....

Almost ~~TO~~ THE *Altar*

Two fun and romantic full-length novels from bestselling authors

USA TODAY Bestselling Author

Christine Rimmer

Leanne Banks

Available everywhere books are sold in February 2004.

Silhouette®
Where love comes alive™

Visit Silhouette at www.eHarlequin.com

BR2ATTA

SILHOUETTE *Romance*

COMING NEXT MONTH

#1710 MAJOR DADDY—Cara Colter
When five adorable, rambunctious children arrived on reclusive Cole Standen's doorstep, his much needed R and R was thrown into upheaval. But just when things were back to the way he liked them (ie. under his control!), Brooke Callan, assistant to the children's famous mother, arrived. Could Brooke and the brood of miniature matchmakers rescue this hero's wounded heart?

#1711 DYLAN'S LAST DARE—Patricia Thayer
The Texas Brotherhood
Pregnant physical therapist Brenna Farren was not going to let her newest patient, handsome injured bull rider Dylan Gentry, give up on his recovery *or* talk her into entering a marriage of convenience with him! But soon she found herself in front of a judge exchanging I dos—and getting a whole different kind of "physical therapy" from her heartthrob husband!

#1712 AN HEIRESS ON HIS DOORSTEP—
Teresa Southwick
If Wishes Were...
Jordan Bishop fantasized about being a princess and living in a palace. But when her secret birthday wish was answered with...*a kidnapping,* she was rescued by the sexiest innocent bystander she'd ever seen. She found herself in his castle—and in the middle of a *big* misunderstanding! Could the love-wary Texas oil baron who saved the day be Jordan's prince?

#1713 THE SECRET PRINCESS—Elizabeth Harbison
The princess was alive! And she was none other than small-town bookstore owner Amy Scott. Despite her protests, Crown Prince Wilhelm insisted the skeptical American beauty return to Lufthania with him. But while Amy was sampling the royal lifestyle, Wil found himself wanting to sample Amy's sweet kisses....

SRCNM0204